Winter's Deception

Book One of the Seasons Series

First published in 2021
by Maida Vale (an imprint of The Black Spring Press Group)

Suite 333, 19-21 Crawford Street
Marylebone, London W1H 1PJ
United Kingdom

Typeset by Subash Raghu
Graphic design by Juan Padron

ISBN 978-1-913606-50-3
www.eyewearpublishing.com

CHAPTER ONE

Simon sat at his desk, and gazed out the window.

From the eighteenth floor, he could make out the nearby tower of Big Ben, as well as the dome of St. Paul's further in the distance. The November afternoon looked miserable and cold. Glum grey rainclouds hung over the sky and steadily drizzled slick, oily rain. Simon watched as the shrill wind battered and lashed the trees in a nearby park. He returned his attention to the office. Two desks away his colleague David checked his phone.

'You know, checking your phone every five minutes isn't going to make the baby come any quicker,' Simon remarked, as he stared at the spreadsheet on the screen in front of him. The chart documented the projected amount of ecological fertilizer required to yield a specific amount of barley per square meter of land for a region in England.

'You're right,' David said. 'It's just she had twinges this morning and is already three days late.' David returned his phone to his pocket and continued poring over a similar spreadsheet on his computer.

'I'll tell you what, it's almost half past five, why don't you go?' Simon said. 'We're nearly finished here anyway.'

'You don't mind?' David asked.

'No, you've been agitated all day, and it's beginning to annoy me,' said Simon. 'I've been trying to get you to concentrate, but I can't be bothered anymore. I give up. Go home and fawn over Lilly.'

'Thanks Simon, you're a mate.' David grabbed his coat and rushed out the door without shutting down his computer.

'Call me as soon as there's news, okay?' Simon shouted after him.

****

Once David left, Simon sat back and smiled. He remembered how he had been when his wife, Helen, awaited their first baby. Jumpy.

He finished calculating the final column on the spreadsheet, shut down his computer and walked over to David's desk to shut down his as well.

'David isn't the only one that wants to go home early tonight,' Simon announced to the now empty office as he took out his phone, sliding his finger across the screen. He had one new text message.

Helen, 17:04

Hi honey, what time are you getting home? I've put William to bed and am preparing special dinner for this evening. Your favourite. Love you xxx

Simon left the office gladly. He took his phone from his pocket and read the message again, slipping it back into his pocket as he entered the station. The train journey home seemed to take forever, even though it was the same thirty minutes as always. As he sat squashed shoulder to shoulder with complete strangers, he composed his reply:

Simon, 17:13

Hey baby, I'm on the train now. Probably another thirty minutes. I'll read William his bedtime story. Then we'll have the evening all to ourselves.;-) xxx

He put the phone back in his pocket and spent the rest of the train journey thinking about his beautiful Helen. Simon managed to jostle through the crowded tube station and escape onto the street, walking as fast as he could without running. He had no idea what would be waiting for him soon.

★★★★

Helen peeled the carrots while sitting at the kitchen table. Her phone lay on the side, where she had left it after Simon's text. Once she had finished, she stood up, took a knife from the rack, and diced the carrots into slices.

'Twenty past five, good, it should be ready about the same time as the chicken.' Helen smiled to herself.

With the vegetables steaming and the potatoes and chicken already in the oven, Helen decided to make a nice relaxing cup of tea. She picked up the kettle and wandered to the sink.

Ding-Dong!

The doorbell chimed as Helen filled the kettle. She looked up. A man's silhouette loomed against the frosted glass. Helen turned the lock and parted the door a small bit. The stranger towered over her at the doorstep. He wore a grey cap and matching overalls.

Wham!

He slammed his shoulder against the door, forcing it open with astonishing violence. Helen flew backwards like a rag doll.

'What the?' Helen spluttered as she attempted to pick herself up – but the stranger in grey had already crossed the threshold. He pressed an evil-looking knife against her fine throat and grabbed her by her hair.

'Stop!' No!' Helen cried as he dragged her towards the kitchen. Helen struggled and kicked with all her strength, but it was no good, she was no match for the intruder.

Four other men followed into the house. The last one closed the door behind him. From outside the house, nothing would seem amiss, cruelly.

Now in the kitchen the assailant hurled Helen towards the table. She stumbled against it, panting, putting her hands out to steady herself. Then she spotted the knife she had used while preparing dinner. She reached for it, a bit hopefully maybe, and took grip of its handle, but was stopped sharp as a cold sensation brushed the base of her skull.

'I wouldn't if I were you. Mine's quite a bit bigger and sharper than yours,' the stranger said with supremely confident irony. Helen winced and released the smaller knife, turning to face her captors; two were in the kitchen with her.

The floorboards creaked overhead as the other three moved about the house.

The stranger held the blade to Helen's throat before sliding it back into the sheath hanging at his side.

Helen watched him carefully. She was intelligent. She was trying to figure out what this was about, who he could be, and how she might make it out alive. She knew her husband would be home soon, and she knew her child was also in the house. It was every mother's nightmare, but she tried to remain calm and collected. *Come on Helen, think!*

The stranger was only slightly taller than her and had a ragged scar under his left eye. His nose was crooked; Helen suspected someone had had the pleasure of breaking it. His hair was shaven close to his scalp, and he wore a smirk that exuded utter contempt and hinted at sadistic tendencies.

The other intruder stood in the corner of the kitchen, leaning arrogantly against the sideboard like he owned the place, which, at that moment, he almost did. He was much taller than the other man, and his thick muscular arms were crossed over his broad chest. He wore grey overalls and his smile was as sickeningly confident as his partner's. Perhaps most notably, both strange men had dark blue skin and deep crimson eyes.

This is bad, she thought.

'There's no sign of him, Lord Malcor.' Another accomplice had entered the kitchen and reported to the man with the scar. *So he is a Lord*.

This third intruder also possessed dark blue skin and crimson red eyes, although his physique was stockier and shorter than Lord

Malcor's. The third intruder wore a set of dark brown combat armour on top of his overalls. Heavy pads guarded his chest, upper arms and thighs while a military-grade pistol remained holstered at his waist.

And for some reason he's looking for my husband. Helen's hand brushed against her pocket where her phone normally was kept, but of course she had left it out when texting. Lord Malcor was not concerned with that useless movement.

'Where is your husband?' Malcor demanded.

'Why the hell would I tell you?' Helen scowled. 'Who are you people? And what do you want with him?' she snarled.

'Answer my question, woman!' Malcor shoved Helen in a most ungentlemanly fashion, sending her staggering backwards.

The men, if such they were, sniggered as another brute entered the kitchen, whose disproportionately long arms and legs matched his long, pointed nose. The lanky intruder also wore body armour but carried no firearms. Instead, his armour was adorned with five assorted and capable-seeming knives.

'There is no sign of him in the house, my Lord. But we did find a child sleeping in one of the rooms,' he informed. 'What should we do with it?' The creature leered at Helen.

'Shall we kill it, my Lord?' One of the others asked from where he was perched by the sink, as if his demented Christmas had come early.

'No!' Helen lunged at Malcor, who stepped easily aside. Years of combat experience laced his movement with confidence and grace. Malcor punched her on her forearm just above the elbow.

Helen cried out as Lord Malcor delivered a second blow. Air wheezed from her lungs. The other men cackled with pleasure at watching her suffer.

'Sit,' Malcor demanded imperiously, as he pushed Helen limply into one of the kitchen chairs. Defeated, clutching her arm, Helen obliged. This was not a situation she could easily wriggle out of.

'No. Our orders were only to kill the adults, we leave the child.'

Malcor turned back to Helen. 'Now you're going to sit in that chair quietly and wait for your husband to get home...and if you try anything else foolish, I'll send one of my men here to kill the child. Do you understand?' Helen nodded.

Tears streaked her face as she sat at the kitchen table, still clutching her arm. Her dislocated bone sent throbbing jolts of pain through her body, while fear surged through her mind. *What next?*

★★★★

Simon reached his front door, grateful that his commute was over and that he could enjoy the weekend. Pushing the door open, Simon entered the house.

'I'm home,' he said. There was no answer.

'Helen? I'm home!' Simon bellowed, as he climbed the stairs and entered William's room. William lay sleeping, already in bed. Simon tiptoed to his son, bent down, and kissed the boy goodnight. He pulled William's blanket back on. The house stood still.

In the kitchen, the intruders waited with Helen, standing motionless. The fifth member of their group, an unremarkable looking individual when compared to the others, crept into the kitchen whilst Simon was upstairs. Malcor put a finger to his mouth, motioning to his crew to stay silent. They waited as he descended the stairs. Two of them took position on either side of the kitchen door.

Simon's footsteps echoed against the hardwood floor as he approached the kitchen. A third man stalked over to where Helen sat, pulling out one of the five knives upon his person as he did so. He positioned himself behind Helen and held the short black blade to her throat.

'Helen, where are you?' Simon called, entering the kitchen.

The trap had been laid. The two men grabbed each of Simon's arms and stomped on his calves. Simon buckled to his knees.

'Get away from my wife!' Simon yelled as Malcor squared up to him with a smirk. Simon wrenched his hand out of one of the men's grip and swung it into the other's gut. The opponent grunted but kept a firm hold of Simon's other arm. Malcor slammed his boot into Simon's face. Simon could taste blood. He touched his nose. It felt disfigured.

'Who we are is unimportant. You, however, are the eminent geneticist Simon Penatome.' Malcor crouched down to level his face with Simon's.

'Yes, what of it?' Simon spoke through his pain.

Malcor's gaze fixed on Simon's eyes which were a depthless, dark emerald green – though Simon slumped in agony, his eyes shone in defiance, that troubled Malcor.

'There's something familiar about you. Have we met before?' Malcor snarled.

'I'm sure I would have remembered your ugly face,' Simon replied.

'Indeed. Well, I would have liked to interrogate you further, it's been so long since I've been allowed to test a Human to their limits,' Malcor hissed, then a sneer pulled at his lips.

'I do remember you, we have met before, King Autumn.' His expression turned triumphant as Simon's eyes widened.

'No...you are mistaken,' Simon stuttered.

'Just think of the glory that will be mine, once the Emperor finds out that I have found and bested the king of the Autumn Elves!'

'Why?' Simon groaned, the pain growing worse; he was also very concerned for his family, as these were truly evil creatures. He sought to remain calm. So long as there was talk there was hope. Not much, he considered, ruefully.

'The Emperor finds your genetic research to be an affront to nature. Anything that helps the disgusting Human species to thrive cannot be tolerated. Your death will set them back by decades. As well as send the humans at FERA an important message that the Dark Elves should not be tested.'

Simon nodded, understanding now, but trying to keep a brave face. 'Quite the rhetoric, although it is rather less meaningful coming from a soldier and not the General in charge. So, tell me who is giving the orders? Who is this Emperor that you serve?' Simon's words were rewarded with a vicious punch making him grunt with pain.

Malcor nodded at one of his men holding Simon, who raised his fist and crashed it against his temple. Helen's scream echoed around the room.

Simon was losing consiciousness, even as Helen continued her banshee wailing, and they were both powerless to do anything now to stop the horrors that they now knew were bound to unfold in this otherwise normal unremarkable home.

****

William sat on the hospital bed. He had been here for a week, since the police and Uncle David had found him.

Through the open door William saw his Godfather, Uncle David. *Everything will be alright now, Uncle David will know where Mummy is,* he thought.

Mummy had said that Uncle David would be a Daddy soon, and that they would be allowed to visit at his house to see the new baby. William closed his eyes in an attempt to force the bad thoughts away.

Uncle David talked in the corridor with the doctors and with the funny woman who had tried to talk to him in sign language when he had first arrived here. She wasn't very good at sign language and some of it had been wrong.

She told William she was a social worker, whatever that was. William smiled while thinking about the woman and her funny sign language. William hoped Uncle David would take him home. Not the home he left; that was gone now, because Mummy did not come back for him...

But why hadn't Mummy come back? Had he been bad? The thoughts made him want to cry again.

He remembered waking up and going downstairs in his house. Mummy wasn't in the kitchen and it smelled like something had been burnt. He waited all day, but no one came, and he couldn't open the door. It had got dark and Uncle David came and called the policemen. They showed him their police car and let him ride with them.

William liked that, until they brought him here to this horrible hospital. But he couldn't stay in the hospital much longer because Mummy would come back to their house and get him, she wouldn't leave him, he was sure of that. He couldn't remember being bad.

William swung his legs at the edge of the hospital bed and waited for Uncle David. Uncle David looked in and smiled sadly.

'I hate this horrid place,' William said, holding up his hands so Uncle David could see he was talking. 'I hate the smell and I hate the food; they don't know what I like to eat like Mummy does. How much longer will they be?' William gestured. 'How long does it take to tell the doctors I can go with you?'

'Not much longer, mate,' David signed back.

'Will Mummy come back? What if she does come back and I'm not there? How would Mummy find me if I'm with you? And what about Daddy?' William signed at his godfather.

'Don't worry, they will know you are with me,' David replied, making sure William could see his hands. David stepped in. William leapt off the bed and hurled himself into David's arms. *What a bloody mess,* David thought to himself as he stroked the boy's head.

'It's okay, Will,' David murmured, knowing that William couldn't hear him. 'You're coming home with me.'

David picked up William and seated the boy on the edge of the bed before him. *Are all four-year-olds this small?* David thought.

William stared at David. He had his father's dark, emerald green eyes. David swallowed, a lump forming in his throat.

'I'm taking you home to live with me. Is that alright with you, William?' William nodded.

'Yes, as long as it's just for a bit, until Mummy and Daddy come and collect me?'

David forced a smile, collected William's bag, and lifted William off the bed. William held Uncle David's hand as they walked through the hospital and along the corridor that led to the car park. William looked up at Uncle David and smiled when he spotted his red car.

David unlocked it and placed William's bag inside before lifting him into the new car seat that was strapped in the back. David passed the boy his favourite teddy. William cuddled it and popped his thumb in his mouth as David kissed his head.

As David started the car, a figure emerged in the rear view-mirror.

'Jeez, Althea,' David gasped, 'I wish you would stop doing that.'

Althea Rosa was a Hollyhock Elf. Her purple hair draped around her shoulders and extended down to her upper arms, perfectly complementing her green-tinted skin and pale yellow eyes.

'You know I can't resist.'

'I did wonder when you were going to make an appearance.' David flicked his gaze away from her, concentrating on the road. 'You're like a little ninja.'

Althea smirked at him and turned to the sleeping child strapped in the car seat beside her. David found the Elf's silence disconcerting given that she usually wasted no time in making her opinions known. David ploughed on anyway: 'Are you going to allow William to see you Al? I think it would help.' David glanced at Althea in the mirror.

Althea nodded. 'Good. In that case you can help us settle him in, and then maybe have a go at becoming his friend.' David stopped at a red light and drummed his fingers on the steering wheel. 'What do you think?'

'The last time you persuaded me to do that it bit me, remember?' Althea pulled a face.

'Well, yeah, but look at him! Isn't he cute?' David raised an eyebrow in the rear-view mirror.

'Oh alright, it might be fun to have my own human boy,' Althea conceded. David sighed and took a left turn into a small country village, passing thatched cottages and the local pub before turning off by the village green. They were almost home.

****

William looked around at his new room; his Aunty Lilly had painted it a forget-me-not-blue colour and pasted stickers of tractors and lorries on the walls. Even though the room contained all the furniture and toys from his old room, the space still seemed foreign.

Uncle David had read him a bedtime story, and now he was waiting for Aunty Lilly to tuck him in. Aunty Lilly was in the other room feeding the baby.

It was a girl. He would have preferred another boy to play with. Girls, in William's opinion, were silly. He didn't understand why they loved all their dolls and pretend tea parties. As he was contemplating ways to get out of playing pretend tea parties, William noticed a different girl sitting on the end of his bed.

She had appeared suddenly. She was wearing pyjamas like his, but she looked different. He realised she had purple hair and her skin was an odd colour as well. She was looking at one of his books. *Where had she come from?* William thought. He was sure she hadn't been there just a minute ago. Maybe she was a ghost…

The strange girl started to giggle. 'I'm not a ghost.' William blinked, *how could she hear his thoughts? And how could he hear her?*

'I'm an Elf!' The girl chuckled. 'Look.' Althea put the book down and pushed her purple hair away from her ears to reveal their pointed tips. She giggled again.

'You're still a girl though. And girls are silly,' William said.

'Oh! Well I was going to be your friend.' Althea pouted. 'But perhaps I won't be now.' As Althea spoke a book tumbled off the shelf.

William looked over at it, confused, and when he looked back, the Elf had vanished.

'Wait, please come back! I'm sorry,' William whispered into the air as Aunty Lilly walked into the room.

'Sorry William, the baby just didn't want to go to sleep.' Aunty Lilly moved her hands so William could see as she spoke. She tucked him in and kissed him on the head. 'Tomorrow we can go and take a look at your new school.' Lilly smiled and stroked his head. 'It's just in the next village, okay?'

As William nodded, he saw something hiding behind Aunt Lilly. It was the little Elf, giggling. What was this? William thought.

Could Aunty Lilly see the Elf? No, grown-ups were rubbish at that sort of thing. William curled up in a ball and put his hands over his ears. He could hear everything, not just Aunty Lilly's voice but lots of sounds, and he didn't know what they were all doing there in his head, crashing around; he had never experienced sound before.

How was he going to get to sleep with all this noise? Before now he hadn't been able to hear anything, the world was always silent and peaceful, but ever since he had come to this place he had been assaulted by a terrifying cacophony of noises.

'Night, William.' Aunty Lilly left the room. The Elf waved at William and skipped after her.

William snuggled down in his bed, as the sounds that he had been so unfamiliar with began to fade back to silence, and despite his original confusion William couldn't help but feel lonely in their absence. *I can figure it all out tomorrow,* he thought, before closing his eyes and drifting to sleep.

★★★★

Downstairs, Lilly found David slumped on his favourite sofa. His hair was ruffled and dark circles creased the skin. David had spent almost the whole week in London, sorting out the paperwork and arrangements for the funeral.

'How was it?' Lilly asked as she sat next to him, curling her legs under her. Lilly enjoyed the warmth of the fire, resting her head against his shoulder.

'Awful, as you would expect. He is convinced Helen is going to come back. How do you tell a four-year-old his mother's dead?' David rubbed his eyes.

'They found her body by the river. There was no sign of Simon, but the police seem to think he's dead as well. They said the blood in the kitchen wasn't Helen's so it was likely Simon's.' David sighed.

'I found William in his bed and I suspect that he had been there for some time. It's only a matter of when not if they find Simon's body, I fear.' David ran his hands through his hair again. 'The worst part was going to the mortuary to identify Helen's body,' David shuddered at the morbid thought.

Lilly hesitated. 'How did she look?'

'Peaceful. The report said that she died from asphyxiation.' Tears ran down David's cheeks. 'I just can't believe they're gone. I knew Helen my entire life.'

Lilly leaned over and kissed David. 'I'm so sorry you had to do that on your own,' she said, fighting her tears. She sought for and found her strength.

'Something must be going on,' David said, peering down at Lilly. 'All these scientists disappearing, and the deaths as well, this whole thing just stinks of Fairy involvement,' he snarled, surprising Lilly.

'I know,' Lilly replied quietly. 'There have been rumours at work for months, but there's no proof. And the Elder Council's pretending nothing's happening. With the new baby I haven't had the time to look into it.' Lilly took a deep breath. 'Right now, we have a small, confused boy asleep upstairs and for his sake we must be as normal as possible,' she declared.

David chuckled, 'Normal? Here? Good luck.'

★★★★

Andarta shifted her gaze from her paperwork as the door to her office opened and Laran shuffled in quietly. He pulled out a spare chair and slumped his tall frame into it.

'I need to leave for a while.' His emerald green eyes reflected hers and travelled over the familiar contours of her face. Her striking red hair accentuated her pale skin and minimal make up.

'Where are you going?' Her eyes drifted over his bruised face, and defeated shoulders. The office felt small with his large frame dominating the space.

'I don't know, but I can't stay here,' Laran lifted his head to look at her. The life had gone out of his eyes.

'You're not well enough. Please, come back with me. You like Canada,' Andarta rose gracefully to her feet. She walked around the desk and knelt in front of him. 'You still have me. You will get over this. Their lives were always fleeting,' her gaze blazed into his as he hung his head, defeated. 'You have to be strong. You're the King.' Andarta brushed his curly auburn hair from his face.

'Please. I can't,' he whispered. 'They're dead. There is nothing here for me now. I'm sorry.' Laran stood and rubbed his face, hoping somehow to draw strength into himself. He sighed and left the room without looking back.

Andarta watched him walk away, the confident, purposeful man she adored was now just a mere memory. A knock at the door pulled Andarta's attention back. A young Autumn Elf put his head round the door.

'Ma'am, we are getting reports of Dark Elf movements in Eastern Europe. Hàlfr sent me, and he says the matter needs your personal attention.'

'Oh, yes, right, just give me a minute.' Andarta nodded as the Elf closed the door. *It doesn't make sense* she thought, *The Dark Elves have been quiet since the war, why come back now?* She pulled a small mirror from her desk drawer and checked her appearance before striding out of the room.

★★★★

'Gaillardia, sweetheart, come on, wake up! There's a good boy.'

Gail slowly opened his eyes to see Mummy's smiling face.

'Good boy. Now come on, put your coat on for Mummy.' Gail sat up. His mother slipped his coat on over his pyjamas and then his shoes, and he grabbed his blanket as she picked him up.

His arms wound round his mother's neck as he buried his face in her hair, letting her familiar scent comfort him.

She hurriedly carried the child down the stairs from his bedroom and into the hallway.

'James what are you doing with that?' as James walked in from the lounge carrying a gun.

'I'm going to go join the defence, you go to the church and wait for me there, do you understand Jasmine?'

Gail had never seen his father like this. He seemed frightened, and that made Gail feel frightened.

'What? No, stay with us, please, you can't leave me, you can't leave your son,' Jasmine argued.

'I'm sorry Jasmine, but I have to do this. I need to give you a chance,' James replied before opening the front door.

'Come on, I'll walk you to the church,' he said as he stepped out into the street.

Now that he was outside, Gail could hear loud banging and cracking noises coming from the hills above the town.

He looked up to see what was making the sound and saw columns of smoke rising from the hilltop. Army tanks flanked the hill, their colour and details obscured by the early morning gloom.

He could tell they were military because of the banging and the flashes of light that came from them as they fired at each other.

Gail and his mother hurried up the street away from the hilltop and towards the church at the heart of town.

As they jostled through the crowds, Gail watched people rushing past them this way and that. They looked frightened: women were carrying crying children and more men with guns were rushing towards the outskirts of town, towards the source of the banging.

'Mummy, what's happening?' Gail asked confused.

'Don't worry baby, Mummy's got you,' she replied as they reached the town square across from the church. It was packed with people milling about. Gail could see the anxiety on their faces, and it made him feel frightened, so he clung to his mother Jasmine tighter, hiding his face in her neck.

'Okay, stay here, I'll be back soon,' James said as he turned to Jasmine.

'Please don't go out there,' Jasmine cried.

'Sweetheart, you know I have to go, I'll be back before you know it, don't worry. I love you. Now take care of the little man for me won't you?' he asked, kissing Gail on the top of her head.

'I love you, too. Be careful, okay? No heroics,' Jasmine pleaded as she kissed him, tears running down her cheeks.

'I'll be careful, I promise,' James shouted, as he pulled away and began to jog up one of the side streets, heading in the same direction as the other men with guns had gone.

The church appeared to be full, so they were forced to stand out in the square.

Jasmine held Gail close to her chest, her hand stroking him on the back in exactly the way he liked.

They stood there for what seemed like hours to Gail, listening to the banging and crackling in the distance, the wailing of children, and the general hubbub of the townspeople.

Suddenly, one of the nearby buildings exploded into flames, forcing Gail to bury his head in Jasmine's chest out of fear. When he looked up again, he could see vehicles had driven up to the square blocking every street.

The trucks were open-topped and had big nasty-looking machine guns mounted on them. They were driven by purple-skinned men with black hair and blood-red eyes.

'Oh no, not Dark Elves,' Jasmine muttered, stepping deeper into the crowd.

One of the purple men, dressed in a long black coat, jumped down from the back of his truck and stepped forwards. Gail could tell by the way he carried himself and the way the others watched him carefully that he was their leader.

'Jasmine and Gaillardia Aristata, step forwards now!' he shouted into the crowd, now stunned into silence.

'Mummy, that's us,' Gail said.

'Shh baby, I know,' Jasmine replied, pressing Gail's head against her chest.

'Jasmine and Gaillardia Aristata step forwards!' the purple man shouted again. Still Jasmine didn't dare move.

'This is your last opportunity! Step forwards now!' He shouted, clearly more and more annoyed. Again, Jasmine refrained from doing what he asked, remaining still, hidden within the crowd.

'Gail my sweet baby if you lose me, you hide do you hear, you hide from these bad men,' Jasmine whispered in Gail's ear, feeling his head bob and his grip tighten around her neck as she kissed him, gazing at the men threatening them.

'Fine, if that's the way you want to play it, don't say I didn't give you a fair chance,' the man called out before turning to the closest tank.

Gail didn't hear what the leader said, but the man he spoke to immediately opened fire on the crowd, with total disinterest in human life.

Jasmine gasped and turned to run, but there was nowhere to go, they were surrounded by Dark Elves, trapped within the vulnerable, milling, Human crowd.

The shouts and screams of terror could hardly be heard over the deafening evil music of relentless gunfire. Gail could feel people pushing and pressing against him as they desperately, hopelessly, tried to escape.

Amidst the confusion Gail was torn from his mother's arms and thrown to the ground.

'Gail!' Jasmine shouted as she attempted to work her way back towards him. She was obstructed by all the terrified people.

Gail had lost sight of his mother, and, in the scrum of the crowd, on the ground, a knee came driving towards him, making direct contact with his nose. Blood splattered his face as another person fell on top of him. He could hear the bullets flying overhead, and dull terrible thuds as they hit the townspeople. Hit them again and again.

Then suddenly, it was over as quickly as it had begun. Massacres are like summer storms sometimes. They blow up out of nowhere and go again just as quickly. The gunfire over, an eerie silence descended over the square, punctuated, all too predictably, by the moaning and crying of the injured and dying. This was terrorism, pure and simple.

'Jasmine and Gaillardia Aristata, if you still live or are in the church, step forward now!' the leader of the Dark Elves shouted again.

He waited a moment, but nobody stepped forward. Gail couldn't see his mother, he couldn't even get out from underneath the heavy person lying on top of him.

'So be it. Finish off the survivors and grenade the church.'

Gail heard glass smashing and the sound of muffled screaming that was immediately silenced by a loud sudden bang.

More smashing and banging sounds followed but Gail couldn't focus on anything other than on the purple men who were gradually getting closer to where he was lying.

Whenever they came across someone moaning or moving, they would stop to shoot them and then move on. No one found moved again after that. This was brutal efficiency. Compassion was absent, like light is in the darkest night. No place for a child.

Gail could hear them coming towards him and instinctively jammed his eyes shut tight, lying as still as he could.

He heard a loud bang as one of the Dark Elves killed someone lying nearby with a direct headshot, clean, precise, definitive.

Gail waited, trembling, but the bang he was dreading most, the one that would signal his end, never came.

Gail didn't know how long he had been lying there, but when he dared to open his eyes, the purple men had gone.

The sun had come up now and birds were singing, their cheerful chirping the only sound that could be heard besides the roar and shifting of the burning church, the house of hope reducing to ash.

Gail struggled out from underneath the dead person on top of him and got to his feet.

He wandered around the square amongst the bodies until he found Mummy. She was lying still on the ground and didn't react when Gail approached her.

Unsure of what else to do, he sat down, snuggled into her side, and went to sleep.

Later, time had no meaning now, someone was coming, he could hear cars. He shook his mother, trying to wake her up, but still she lay motionless.

'Gail...Gaillardia, Jasmine please answer.' Gail sat up and looked around at the sound of his name.

The air smelled of smoke and something else he had never noted before. The dead. He thought he recognised the voice and then his hunch was confirmed when he saw his grandfather running into the square before stopping with a gasp.

The grandfather's keen eyes surveyed the carnage until they spotted Gail. Moving toward Gail, his face paled as he saw Jasmine's body. Kneeling he held out his arms to Gail who swiftly moved into the embrace.

'Granddad, Mummy won't wake up!' Gail inhaled the familiar scent of his granddad as his lip quivered and his eyes filled with tears.

'I know my precious boy, I know,' his granddad's arms were too tight, making Gail squirm until he placed him back on his feet.

The boy reached out and held his grandfather's hand.

The sound of engines filled the air, their headlights shining in the light, creating silhouettes out of their occupants.

'Gaillardia?' Someone was calling his name, and he looked up to find his uncle Hàlfr striding towards him. 'Gaillardia, you are safe, thank God,' Hàlfr shouted, grinning at him as he walked nearer.

'Lord Bracken, I'm surprised to see you here so quickly,' Hàlfr narrowed his eyes as he addressed Gail's grandfather.

'I was on my way to celebrate Gail's birthday tomorrow, a moment earlier and I would have been caught up in it.'

'How fortunate for you, perhaps even a little too fortunate?' Hàlfr replied with a scowl.

'How dare you insinuate that I would kill my own daughter. I knew you Autumn Elves were foolish, but this is a new level of stupid.'

'Perhaps not, I can't imagine even Dark Elves are psychotic enough to knowingly attack their own,' Hàlfr conceded begrudgingly. 'Unless of course the Emperor knows about Gail?' Hàlfr continued.

'And how would he know that, apart from myself there is barely anyone else who knows about Gail's true lineage. They must have just got lucky attacking a random Autumn Elf town that Gail just happened to be in,' Lord Bracken mused, before continuing, 'which is why I said that we should raise him as a Dark Elf, it would be far safer, especially now.'

Gail observed that a lady he did not recognise had climbed out of one of the vehicles talking rapidly on her phone before shoving it roughly into her coat pocket, as she now listened to the conversation between Hàlfr and Granddad.

'Absolutely not, the Autumn Lords were reluctant enough to accept the peace terms as it is, if they find out about this there will be all out war again,' the lady stated, in a soft authoritative voice.

'So, we just hush it up and pretend it never happened? Andarta you can't be serious?' Hàlfr asked with indignation.

'Yes Hàlfr, I mean look at all this. Why would the Dark Elves attack like this? The war is over.' Queen Andarta stood still and gazed at the wreckage around her. Gail watched tentatively, he didn't understand what the adults were talking about and was beginning to feel cold and sleepy.

'There are still those who don't recognise the peace treaty, and those who resent Lord Aristata for the heavy toll he forced on them during the war. I wouldn't be surprised if this was done out of revenge,' Lord Bracken replied.

Hàlfr moved around, looking at each of the bodies. 'What I don't understand is why leave him here? Where is Lord Aristata anyway?' Hàlfr asked as one of his lieutenants walked over to him.

'Sir, we have located Lord Aristata on the eastern edge of town,' he declared.

'Excellent,' Hàlfr responded.

'I'm afraid he didn't make it, sir,' the lieutenant said grimly.

'Oh. I see. Thank you, lieutenant,' Hàlfr replied, his face falling and his gaze returning to Gail, a frown etched between his eyes.

'Well we can't leave Gail here, he is the last Aristata.' Andarta gazed at the boy and sighed. Gail watched as she walked over to him, knelt down on the cobbled stones of the square, and smiled.

'I think we should keep his survival a secret, for now,' Hàlfr remarked as he moved through the pile of bodies, inspecting their wounds, shaking his head.

'I am inclined to agree with you, this doesn't sit right,' Lord Bracken replied as he picked Gail up.

'Pair that with the murder of Helen, it seems too convenient to be a coincidence. Something more is going on here.' Andarta shifted her gaze back to the little boy as she gracefully rose to her feet.

'Laran's wife is dead, what of the son!?' Lord Bracken demanded, his face stricken at this news.

'He survived and is safely hidden away. Bracken, Gail can't go with you, you know that.' Andarta gazed at Lord Bracken, her expression softening at his distress.

'So, this is it, I lose my daughter and grandson on the same day? The point was that he would unite the Elven houses, how will that be possible if he is raised in secret and nobody knows?' He grunted with a scowl.

'This has to stay with us, his survival depends on it. I will raise him in a way so that no questions will be asked.' Andarta paced, a frown creasing her brow. 'I will release a press statement stating I have adopted a war orphan.'

'What about Laran, he will never go along with this,' Hàlfr gazed at Andarta and Lord Bracken.

'Laran does not need to know Gail's true heritage. I will remove Gail from the Elf World until he is ready to know the truth.'

Andarta gazed down at the small boy whose future they were discussing. Gail looked in turn at the pretty lady, rubbing his blanket against his nose.

'Gail, this is Andarta, Queen Autumn, you can go home with her, if you like,' Hàlfr said, stroking Gail's hair gently.

'Can't I go with Granddad?' confusion etching his features as tears welled in his eyes.

'No sweetheart your granddad can't look after you,' Andarta smiled.

'Can Mummy come as well?' Gail turned his head to look at Hàlfr.

'No, my brave boy, Mummy and Daddy can't be with you anymore,' his grandfather answered, placing him on his feet. Squatting down he smiled at Gail. 'Andarta is going to be your mummy now, okay?'

Gail looked up at Andarta, *she didn't look like his mummy, why did he have to go with her?* Gail thought to himself frightened at the prospect.

Gail gasped as Andarta hugged him tight, tears streaming down her face. She smelled nice, sort of flowery, like Mummy he thought. He could feel a dampness on his shoulder as Hàlfr lifted him up in strong arms. Andarta rose to her feet and stepped away, wiping her face.

'I'm sorry Hàlfr,' she choked out, walking back to the car.

And so it was that events were set in motion…

CHAPTER TWO

Fourteen years later, present day

Gail checked his phone. He expected his father to pull up at the house in five minutes. He scanned round the room of his flat for any stray belongings one last time, before picking up his assortment of bags and placing them outside his door.

'You off?' Sara asked, as she clattered down the stairs, coming to a stop next to him.

'Oh, um, yeah, my dad will be here soon to collect me,' Gail smiled at her.

'I'll miss you!' Sara flung her arms around him and kissed him on the cheek. 'Bye Gail,' Sara said, as she walked out the front door.

'Bye Sara.'

Gail locked the entrance behind him and shoved the keys in an envelope, scribbling his name and flat number on the front. He slid the envelope through the letter box as instructed by his landlord. He picked up the bags and walked down the flight of steps to the sun-dappled street below.

Happiness and regret painted his mood as he surveyed the street, unsure of what to do with the final moments of his time at Harvard University. Gail had spent four happy years here. His short dark auburn hair ruffled in the breeze. He ran his hand through it, styling it with his fingers to the side, in the fashion he preferred: it framed his face and highlighted his straight nose and slightly full mouth. His dark chocolate brown eyes surveyed the world with a keen intellect. At nineteen years of age, Gail was one of Harvard University's youngest graduates in Economics and Finance. He was graduating at the top of his class.

Gail took off his navy sports jacket and rolled up his shirt sleeves. He slung the jacket over his shoulder and brushed a loose thread off his navy chino trousers. Four years of university hockey and squash had sculpted Gail's six-foot frame into a well-muscled physique. He sighed and checked his phone once more. Two more minutes.

Gail's mouth curved into its usual smile as a sleek, silver Jaguar cruised down the street toward him. The car slid to a stop at the curb where Gail stood. A man with curly auburn hair, striking dark emerald green eyes, and skin the colour of warm honey, just like Gail's, climbed out of the car with the fluid movement of someone at total ease with their body.

Dressed in smart grey trousers and a shirt, he wrapped Gail in a spine-crushing hug.

'Dad, it's good to see you, too,' Gail managed to say once he was released.

'Hop in, son,' Laran said. 'Your mother is very excited that you're coming home.'

Gail sat in silence and looked through the windscreen as his father effortlessly drove through the city and towards Boston airport where their private jet awaited.

'So, what are your plans now you're finished with university?' Laran asked.

'Oh, I'm not entirely sure. I've had a few job offers from some American investment firms...and Cousin Eric has invited me to join his firm in Sydney. But I don't know, I could use a little downtime to relax, if I'm honest,' Gail replied, observing the traffic around them. He grinned as a lady in a Mercedes admired first the car and then the man behind its wheel. Laran concentrated on the lights changing.

'Well you are certainly not going to Eric's,' Laran scoffed. 'Why don't you work with me for a bit until you decide? I have a little problem you might enjoy solving.'

'Oh, that does sound intriguing. Anyway, what's wrong with Eric? I thought you liked him?' Gail glanced at his father, and then returned his attention to the traffic. The shops and residential buildings had now given way to industrial structures.

'I do like him,' Laran said. 'I think all the trouble he causes Ash is hilarious, and I especially like the way he is so adept at spending all of Ash's money.' Laran flicked the left indicator on and turned the car down another road. 'But I most certainly do not enjoy the idea of you hanging around him for too long and getting your own ideas about leading some devil-maycare playboy lifestyle.'

Gail put his hand over his mouth and pretended to yawn so he could hide his amusement.

You're a sharp lad, and I expect more of you.'

'Oh, okay,' Gail grinned and lapsed into silence. Laran stopped the car at the gate to show a guard his pass.

'Have a nice flight, Mr Autumn,' the guard said, waving them through. Laran drove over to the private hanger where their private jet was waiting.

Gail climbed out to stretch his legs. 'It's a beaut,' Gail said, appreciating the plane. Laran put the bags down next to Gail and draped an arm around his son's shoulders.

'I gave the pilot the night off. Thought you might like to fly her home to Fort Nelson.'

'Really? Amazing! Thanks!' Gail beamed and bolted up the steps into the plane.

****

William stood in the garden leaning against a very old, very large horse chestnut tree in the middle of the ancient wood that surrounded his house. He had spent many happy hours here as a child collecting conkers, spying on and hiding from his little sister. He brushed his curly, messy, auburn hair out of his dark, emerald green eyes and peered around the tree to double check he was alone.

'William, what are you doing?' Althea asked as she walked up to him.

'I'm hiding from the girls, they've been annoying me all day,' William explained, smiling sheepishly at her. They won't leave me alone. I'm being hunted.'

William sighed before grinning at Althea. He could see she was trying not to laugh. 'It's not funny, you know,' he huffed.

'Well it kind of is. I mean look at you, how tall are you now? Six-one? Hiding from two girls is a bit pathetic, for a strapping eighteen-year-old, don't you think?'

'Six-*two,* actually, and when you put it like that, maybe...But they're not just two girls, are they? They got me cornered earlier in greenhouse two and Dad just left me. Can you believe that? Anyway, one of them tried to kiss me!' William's voice tilted into a squeak.

Althea hid her smile, noticing that William was so agitated that he was signing with his hands.

'Here come and sit with me,' Althea pointed to a rotten log on the edge of the clearing.

'Queen Winter will be here in a moment.' Althea took his hand and pulled him down next to her to wait. Across the clearing Lilly came into view, making her way through the trees along a barely visible path.

'I'll protect you,' Althea giggled. A gentle flurry of snow began to fall, and William looked around them.

'Why is Queen Winter visiting?' William asked.

'Oh, something to do with her husband and King Summer I think.'

William looked in the direction of the snow, to the other side of the clearing, where Queen Winter stood. 'She is stunning,' William murmured as he gazed at the Queen of the Winter Fairies.

Althea giggled, 'Yep, and she is way out of your league.' Queen Winter was speaking to his Aunt Lilly, her long silver-white hair hanging loosely down to the small of her back. She had a pale complexion and wide, piercing, icy eyes.

'William, you're drooling,' Althea nudged him in the ribs. 'Still got a crush on her then?' she giggled.

'What? No, I'm not,' William muttered, looking away to hide the slight flush staining his cheeks.

It always snowed when Queen Winter was upset about something and, judging by the rapid gesticulations she was making now, William decided she must be very upset. The snow came down ever harder, and icicles began to form on the branches of the trees, and in William's hair.

Althea shivered, moving closer to William's side. He automatically put his arm around her, trying to keep her warm while brushing snow out of his messy hair with the other hand. He wished he had brought a coat or sweater. But why would he? It was August, after all, and so far, it had been particularly hot. Althea shivered again and snuggled closer.

'What are they talking about anyway? I don't speak Elvish,' William complained.

'If you pay attention, I can translate for you. I'm going to have to put what she is saying in your head telepathically, so it makes sense contextually, so concentrate. No stray thoughts about girls, okay?' Althea took hold of his hand.

'Yes, alright, no need to be so bossy. You know I love that about you, that you enable me to hear. Right, I have cleared my mind,' William grinned cheekily. Althea punched him on the arm. She wasn't translating because he was deaf, not this time anyway. Althea squinted at Queen Winter and Lilly through the opaque wall of snowflakes as they spoke in quick fire Snow Elf. 'Queen Winter is very angry at Taranis, King Winter.'

'What's she saying now Althea? Something must be seriously wrong,' William slurred through chattering teeth. The cold air congealed his thoughts and words.

'Something about spring being late and that Hyperion, King Summer isn't attending to his duties, so Alectrona, Queen Summer, is struggling to keep control,' Althea replied, her teeth chattering almost as much as William's. 'She's saying…she should be in Australia at the moment, but felt she needed to update Lilly on the current situation. She's worried Taranis is meeting with Hyperion and that he may start neglecting his duties as well.' Althea's petite body was struggling to cope with the cold, and her normally green-tinted skin had turned a distinct blue colour.

The snow began to lessen as the two women shook hands and hugged, then with a last flurry of snow Queen Winter vanished and Aunt Lilly turned and walked slowly towards William and Althea. 'Thank goodness that's finished,' William said.

'I can't feel my hands and feet. How are you doing, Althea?' William stood and scooped Althea up in his arms. Her body was so affected by the cold that she could no longer form words. Summer Elves didn't do too well in snowy conditions. William's hands and feet tingled as the feeling gradually returned to them. 'No frost bite today, at least,' William said as he held Althea to his chest so she would warm up. 'That would have taken some explaining at the doctor's.'

'You do worry about daft things.' She hugged him tighter.

'I am so sorry. That went on much longer than I thought it would,' Lilly said. 'Let's get you two back to the house and warm you up.' William and Althea nodded, deeply pleased with that idea.

'William, were you hiding from the twins again?' Lilly asked.

'Um, well, yeah. They just won't leave me alone!' Lilly smiled at his awkward teenage concerns.

Now that Queen Winter had gone, the warm August sunshine streamed into the forest, melting the snow away. At that very moment, Taranis, the King of the Winter Fairies, quickened his pace along the long stone corridor, one of many in his Scottish castle. A thick, plush carpet decorated the hallway's floor and oil paintings hung on the walls. Every five or six pompous steps Taranis would pass a suit of armour as he made his way towards the entrance hall. He stepped haughtily into the room through one of the side doors to see Hyperion, King Summer, sitting on his throne. *Is there no end to his arrogance?* King Winter fumed to himself as he approached Hyperion.

Hyperion was inspecting something beneath his fingernails. He exuded the weary air of someone who had been waiting for hours, although Taranis knew he had only arrived at the entrance hall less than ten minutes before.

King Hyperion stood above the height of most men. Golden hair framed his handsome face and golden flecks ornamented his dark brown eyes. He wore a cream suit on top of a pale blue shirt.

'Taranis, my good man,' Hyperion flashed his white teeth and sprang from the throne to shake King Winter's hand.

What does he want? Taranis thought. *He's never this nice.*

'King Summer – it's good to see you,' said Taranis, 'Although I must confess, I was surprised when you called me. I haven't heard from you for a long time, and, as a matter of fact, I was unaware you had my number,' Taranis replied with a tight smile.

'I still have my sources, brother – and as for where I've been, why don't we discuss it over a drink?' Hyperion replied breezily.

'Yes, let's,' said Taranis 'Please come to my study and tell me more about this mysterious proposition you mentioned over the phone.' Taranis led King Summer unctuously out of the main hall. They passed various ornate tapestries until they reached Taranis' study. Filing cabinets ran along one wall, while a computer screen was mounted on another. The monitor showed one of the various stock indexes. *Probably the FTSE 100,* Hyperion thought to himself, though he could not tell for certain, and didn't much care. A large, masculine oak desk sat in the centre of the room, dominating the space. Beyond the desk a tall picture window provided an impressive view of the castle's perfectly maintained lawns.

Taranis sat in his high-backed leather chair. He motioned towards a notably smaller chair for Hyperion, who took the seat silently, still smiling at Taranis.

'Care for a scotch?' Taranis tugged open a drawer in his desk and pulled out a bottle of single malt and two glasses.

Hyperion nodded in reply. Taranis poured a measure of the honey-brown liquid into each glass.

'You're being very aloof, Hyperion. What is this big proposition you have for me?' Taranis passed King Summer his glass.

'King Winter – ' Hyperion paused and sipped his whiskey. 'Can I ask you a question?'

'Of course.' Taranis said.

Hyperion fixed Taranis with his unwavering gaze.

'Do you like the Humans?'

'What?' Taranis gazed back.

'Do you…like…the Humans?'

'I, don't have...er...a problem with them,' Taranis replied, confused at the sudden seriousness of Hyperion's tone.

'Why?' Hyperion's brow furrowed.

'What do you mean why?' Taranis picked up his glass and took a sip, placing the glass back down. 'Because they have never given me cause to.' He picked a piece of non-existent lint off his trousers, avoiding Hyperion's insistent gaze.

'You mean pollution doesn't upset you? The fact that your kingdom in the North Pole is rapidly shrinking doesn't upset you?' Hyperion looked at him intently.

'Of course, it does, but I don't see what I can do about it.' Hyperion slowly placed his glass on the desk and looked directly at Taranis.

'What if I were to suggest that we killed them? Each and every one of them,' Hyperion said, his voice laced with a chilling tone. Taranis couldn't help but laugh in surprise. Hyperion leaned forward, a zealous gleam in his eyes.

'With them gone we can fix the damage they've done to the planet and set everything right. Reverse global warming, end plant and animal extinction, replant the rain forests. Repair the damage done to your kingdom from oil spills.'

Taranis' eyes widened 'Are you – are you mad? We can't just kill them all. That's ridiculous.' Taranis slammed his glass down and stood up. 'If you're here just to waste my time, then I suggest you leave. You have been away in some weird sort of self-imposed exile for decades and you come back with this idiocy?!' Taranis took a moment to contain his rage. 'This better not be one of your ridiculous jokes.'

'Okay, we don't have to kill all of them – just enough that they won't stand in our way while we repair the damage they've done.' Hyperion raised himself up to face his brother and clasped his shoulders. 'Think about it, it's just like managing a herd of animals. When there are too many, like there are right now, you just reduce their numbers back to a sustainable level.'

Taranis removed Hyperion's hands from his arms and sank back into his chair, rubbing his eyes.

'Even if I did agree to go along with this,' Taranis said 'which I'm not going to do, by the way, how would you do it? We couldn't create a natural disaster powerful enough to do that kind of damage, they have stockpiles and supplies, new technology and resources. The hottest, driest summer or the coldest, harshest winter couldn't do it.' Taranis stopped to collect his thoughts. 'And even if we tried, Mother Nature and the rest of the Council would stop us.'

Hyperion looked across the lawn before slowly turning towards Taranis.

'And what about Laran? He would never go along with it, regardless of what Mother Nature said.' Taranis spluttered, incredulous.

Hyperion smiled. 'But what if we could convince Mother Nature to help us? Laran can always be removed.'

Taranis blinked rapidly in astonishment and poured another measure of whiskey in each of their glasses. He gulped his own down in one and poured himself another. 'What makes you think you could ever convince her? She *is a* Human after all. She wouldn't betray her own kind.'

'What if we had leverage that forced her to help us, willingly or not?' Hyperion sat down and picked up his glass with disconcerting calm. 'What if we compelled her?'

'Compell her?' Taranis' eyebrows shot up. 'With what? What could we possibly use against her?'

'The children, of course,' Hyperion said. 'We'll use the children.' Hyperion leaned back in his chair and clasped his hands behind his head, a wry smile on his face.

Taranis couldn't tear his eyes away from Hyperion's smugness. His long fingers twisted the glass on his desk round and round as everything Hyperion was suggesting sped through his mind. The reports he had read on the new Mother Nature had indicated she was weak, sentimental, possibly foolish, not at all like her mother or grandmother. His Lords had been complaining for a while about the state of the North and South Poles. Perhaps this *was* the solution.

'So how exactly do we capture and hold onto the children? We would need support from one of the other houses, the Winter Elves alone can't capture, let alone hold, the Child of Nature going against Mother Nature and any of the other houses that might help her!' Taranis whined.

'We'll have help, I haven't just been wandering aimlessly all those years. I've been to see the Emperor of the Dark Elves, he has pledged their support,' Hyperion replied.

'The Dark Elves, are you mad? We can't trust them!' Taranis exclaimed in outrage.

'They are just as angry about how the peace treaty has turned out as you or I. Who do you think has suffered the most as a result of the Human's aggressive over-expansion and ceaseless pollution? They can't blend in or integrate like the Spring and Autumn Elves, can they? And at the rate that the Humans are going, they are running out of places to hide,' Hyperion responded, raising his voice to emphasize his point.

'I still have misgivings about working alongside those traitors, but with their help, this crazy plan of yours might just work,' Taranis announced before downing the rest of his scotch.

CHAPTER THREE

Willow lay in the field behind her house, enjoying the summer sun. She listened to the chatter and hum of the various insects and animals who called the grassy field home. An old herbal remedies book lay open next to her. She had enjoyed reading about poultices to cure stings and bites, but now she was bored. Jacen, Willow's best friend, was late.

To make matters worse, Heli, Willow's Summer Elf, was trying to teach some daisies to dance, and Willow was finding this very distracting, albeit highly amusing.

In the distance, she spotted Jacen as he ambled across the field towards her. Willow turned her attention back to Heli and her dancing daisies to find that the Elf had now also enticed some buttercups to join in.

'Woah, Jacen looks hot,' said Heli as she abandoned her daisies and buttercups to watch the boy walk across the meadow.

'You think?' Willow said, *don't blush, don't blush* she chanted in her head.

Heli narrowed her eyes at Willow. 'Err, yeah. I do think.'

'I hadn't noticed,' Willow gazed intently at her book, trying to look engrossed.

Heli smirked and turned the book the right way up. 'Oh, don't give me that, I know you far too well.'

'Okay he *does* look...well-built, but this is Jacen: we grew up together, we sit next to each other in class, sit next to each other at lunch – we even get ill together,' Willow sighed. 'It just feels wrong, you know, thinking about him like that...he's seen me naked! Okay, so that was when we were four, but still. It would be like me fancying William. It would just be wrong. Wouldn't it?' Willow crossed her arms over her chest and hugged herself, biting her bottom lip, swamped with indecision.

'Really?' Heli frowned at Willow. 'Well, I think William is cute.'

Willow stared at Heli and blinked twice 'You think William is cute?'

Heli shrugged, 'Yeah, a bit, he's gotten pretty buff lately, and with all that brooding silence – I think he's interesting,' Heli smirked as Willow shook her head in disbelief.

'Heli he is silent because he is deaf,' Willow shook her head in disbelief.

'But you like Jacen, don't you? I mean *like,* like him?' Heli grinned as she got the conversation back on track.

'Yeah. I suppose, but what if he doesn't like me?' Heli's eyes widened. 'Of course, he likes you!'

'Yes, I know he likes me, as a friend, obviously. But what if that's it. How do I know if he wants *more,* without embarrassing both of us?' Willow let her shoulders slump and fiddled with the ends of her hair. 'He is my best friend it's like I am breaking a code you know.'

'Ah, right, I understand now,' Heli chewed her bottom lip as she watched Jacen approach. She returned to her daisies while she thought about Willow's dilemma. 'Well, on the plus side, at least he doesn't think you're weird,' Heli said with glee.

'That *is* a plus. Gee, thanks, Heli,' Willow flicked her hair over her shoulder and turned away.

'You're welcome,' Heli giggled.

'What took you so long?' Willow asked Jacen as he approached. She narrowed her eyes and crossed her arms but couldn't help smiling.

'Those blasted twins. Who would have thought a shopping trip with Mum could turn into such a drama. In the end I told Mum I would have tea at your house and refused to go with them.' Jacen brushed his floppy, dirty blonde hair out of his hazel eyes.

'Jacen, do you think I'm weird?' Willow asked, ignoring Heli's exaggerated sigh.

Jacen pulled the strap of his bag over his head and dropped it on the ground next to Willow, flopping down in the grass to watch Heli and her dancing flowers. 'No, I don't think you're weird. Why? Have those girls been bullying you again?' A touch of anger had crept into his voice.

'No, no I just...' Willow trailed off.

'Well, sometimes you are a *bit* weird,' Jacen replied, relieved. 'But in a nice way. I mean I like that about you. Why do you ask?' Jacen knotted his brows.

Willow shrugged 'I just wondered, that's all. Jacen, you know how we've known each for, like, forever.'

'Yeah,' Jacen replied slowly, wondering where she was going with this.

'Jacen, do you think I'm pretty?' Willow blurted out, still ignoring Heli, who was rolling her eyes and stifling her laughter.

Jacen rolled over on to his stomach and propped his chin on his arms. He looked at Willow.

'Um, yeah, I think you're pretty,' Jacen tried to keep a straight face while Willow stared at him with her intense grey eyes.

'Why?'

'What do you mean,' Jacen frowned.

'Why do you think I'm pretty,' Willow held his gaze.

'Um, well...you have amazing eyes.'

'What else?'

'I don't know, you just are. I haven't thought too much about it,' Jacen grinned at her.

'Sorry, sorry, I've embarrassed you, I shouldn't have put you on the spot like that,' Willow apologised as Heli sighed loudly.

'Um, well, when you smile there's a little dimple that appears on your chin. It's cute.' *Right underneath that lovely mouth I want to kiss,* he thought, noticing Heli giggle. *Heli get out of my head!* he warned, making Heli giggle more. Jacen frowned.

'Thanks, Jacen, I, um, think you're handsome too,' Willow beamed at him, while Heli pretended to put her fingers down her throat and be sick. Jacen looked away to hide his flushed cheeks.

'What are you reading?' he asked, clearing his throat.

'Oh! It's a book on herbal remedies and their application in medicine. My Gran gave it to me when I last visited. She thought I might find it interesting since I was watching that programme about Early Medicine when she last visited.' Willow opened the book to show Jacen a recipe. 'We could try this one? It's for boils.'

'Oh, gross. You know Willow, and I don't want to sound rude, but your Gran is bonkers. I mean, don't get me wrong, I love her. But in what universe is a book like that suitable reading for a fifteen-year-old?' Jacen laughed.

'Well, to be fair, it probably isn't suitable, but it's quite a lot of fun. Heli thinks most of the plants for this can be found down by the stream, and that this bit of the stream has a resident Sprite that is quite friendly...if you're interested,' Willow said, taking his hands in hers and gazing into his eyes.

'Of course, I'm interested! Who wouldn't be? Lead the way,' Jacen said 'After all, I've never met a Sprite.'

'Oh good, I was feeling really hot sitting here. And I brought us a packed lunch,' Willow grinned, letting go of his hands. Jacen climbed to his feet, pulling Willow up. Her hands rested on his upper arms, and she felt his strong muscles tense.

'Thanks.' Her voice was breathy as she gazed up at him: he was a good head taller than her.

'You're welcome,' he whispered, his mouth a hairs's breadth from hers.

'Come on you two,' Heli shouted from farther down the field, causing them to spring apart. Jacen grabbed his bag and swung it over his head before sprinting after Heli.

'Hey Heli, don't trip,' Jacen laughed as he reached for her arm, trying to pull her over.

'Don't you trip,' Heli giggled, hooking her leg round his.

'I won't,' Jacen wrapped his strong arms around her waist and picked her up in one swift motion. He carried her a few steps before putting her down, laughing.

'That's cheating,' Heli giggled as she tried to walk, wobbling and trying to regain her balance. Tripping over a large mole hill, she flung her arms out and grabbed Jacen, pulling him down with her. They lay laughing in a tangled heap of arms and legs.

'You two are ridiculous.' Willow stepped around them, trying not to laugh. Laughing would encourage them and they really didn't need any encouragement.

'Sorry Willow,' Jacen and Heli giggled while they untangled their legs.

After a few steps, Willow realised she could no longer hear them. As she turned around, she realised she couldn't actually hear anything at all. Willow wondered briefly if this was how it was for William when Althea wasn't around.

Not a bird or insect, not even the wind in the trees, made a whisper. The sun was shining, and the skies looked clear, but Willow felt cold. The chill seeped to her bones. She began to sweat and tremble, paralyzed with fear.

Then Willow heard a low hum. The hum grew louder and louder until it became a thrumming buzz. Willow felt as though she was standing in an angry swarm of bees. Cold beads of sweat rolled down her forehead and the back of her neck as she clasped her palms against her ears. It was futile. Her breath quickened and her knees buckled in terror. She toppled to the ground.

The buzzing stopped. The birds sang again, and the sun's warmth beamed down on her face. Willow shook and lay in the grass until her breath stopped rasping.

'Willow!' Jacen shouted. 'Are you alright?' Jacen ran over to her, Heli close behind. He tossed his bag to the ground and knelt beside Willow's quivering body. His hazel eyes peered at her face from under knitted brows.

'What happened? You look so pale.' He chewed his lip and brushed his hair away from his face. Heli had now caught up with them and sank down next to Willow, putting her arms around her as she hugged her tight.

'I...I don't know,' Willow stuttered. 'I was walking, then everything went silent and cold and there was this terrifying buzzing in my head that got really intense. Then it suddenly stopped.'

'Are you okay now?' Jacen asked. 'Can you walk? Do you want to carry on? I have some chocolate in my bag. We could stop for a bit. I wonder what caused it...We didn't hear anything, did we, Heli?' Jacen gasped.

'Am I rambling?' Both girls nodded. 'Sorry, you just scared me.' Jacen forced a weak smile and brushed back a mop of blonde hair from his eyes. His hand was shaking.

'I'm okay, honestly,' Willow said. 'I'm just a little freaked out, that's all.' She rubbed her sweating palms on her jeans. 'I don't know what that was, and I don't know why it happened only to me.'

'Well, maybe you are weird after all.' Jacen took hold of Willow's arms and pulled her up with him as he stood. He held her close for a minute before stepping back and giving her one of his lopsided grins. Willow looked away in silence. *Maybe I am,* she thought.

'Ok, let's carry on down to the stream,' Willow said, as she held out her hand to help Heli up.

Willow could see the sunlight glinting off the water and the faint gush as the stream flowed over the rocks and around tree roots. Jacen picked up his bag. He narrowed his eyes and surveyed the meadow.

'I'm just checking for anything abnormal,' Jacen shouted to them as he slung his bag over his shoulder and followed the girls.

Heli found her Water Sprite. The Sprite, when not moving, was quite hard to distinguish from the rest of the weeds in the stream, but now that it had come up to them, Jacen noticed that it was actually a lot like a mermaid. Jacen watched fascinated as Heli put her face in the water and blew bubbles.

'Willow, come look!' Jacen said, trying to keep the excitement out of his voice.

'Um, do you mind if I just sit here for a bit in the shade?' Willow sat down leaning against a very large tree.

'No, that's cool,' Jacen said, still watching Heli and the Sprite.

Once Heli and the Sprite had finished exchanging gossip, Heli introduced the Sprite to Jacen.

'Jacen, you can come over now,' Heli waved her hand at Jacen as he slowly walked over.

Stopping on the bank, he couldn't help but stare as he slowly knelt down next to Heli. The Sprite was smaller than Heli. Instead of skin, her tiny body was covered with silver fish scales that shimmered in the sunlight. She had very large almond-shaped eyes, a flat nose, and long green hair that reminded Jacen of fine pond weed. At least he assumed it was her hair. She was surrounded by lots of vegetation, and he couldn't be sure.

'Hi, I'm Jacen, what's your name?'

'I'm Sheila,' the Sprite replied with an innocent smile.

'I've never met a Sprite before…you're awesome.'

'And I've never met a Human boy before.' Sheila narrowed her eyes and looked at Jacen's feet. 'What's wrong with *your* flippers?'

'What do you mean what's wrong with them?' Jacen asked, taken aback.

Heli climbed out of the stream and went and sat with Willow while Jacen talked to the Sprite.

'So, what was that really about?' She gazed at Willow.

'I'm not sure, but I think it's to do with me gaining my gifts.' Willow looked across the meadow and, taking Heli's hand, she concentrated on the bees above her head. As Willow focused, she realised she could understand their humming. It seemed like they were giving each other instructions.

Willow concentrated even more until she could make out what they were saying. Each bee was passing on information about where the best-nectar flowers could be found. The buzzing of the bees had started to make sense. 'Did you hear that?' Willow gazed at Heli, waiting for her response.

'Yeah, when did this start?'

'Last week when I was sitting in the garden, it wasn't as intense as it was just now, and the cold is a new thing.' Willow turned to Heli, her bottom lip caught between her teeth, 'I could hear all these voices, but I was alone. It took me a while to work out what they were. It didn't feel as menacing as it did just now.' Willow tried to hide how anxious she felt about it all. 'I *am* weird,' she whispered. *Why would Jacen want more with me, his freaky little friend,* she thought as her mood soured.

'No, you're not. We should talk to Lilly.'

'No, not Mum, she'll just fuss and crowd me wanting to know everything, you know what she's like.' Willow watched Jacen and the Sprite talking.

'They aren't joined up,' Sheila said.

'You mean, why aren't they webbed?' Jacen asked, and Sheila nodded her head. 'None of my fingers or toes are webbed,' he replied.

'But, then, how do you *swim?*' Sheila asked, brushing her pondweed hair with her flippers. She removed a small fish from it and ate it, her big almond eyes blinking.

'Well, I'm not aquatic. So, I don't, really,' Jacen replied.

'That's weird,' Sheila said, obviously fascinated. Heli wandered down to the stream to see the Sprite again and check on Jacen. Sheila let go of Jacen's hands and turned her attention to Heli.

'Your flippers aren't webbed either. But you're not a Human, you're an Elf.' Sheila examined Heli's hands as they rested in her flippers.

'Elves don't really swim either,' Heli smiled.

'You guys are so weird.' Sheila did a back flip in her excitement, soaking Jacen while Heli escaped by jumping back onto the bank. Willow burst out laughing at the shocked look on Jacen's face. Heli flopped down next to Willow.

'I can hear the animals as well. Over by the gate, the rabbits are discussing the whereabouts of Mrs. Thomas's cat. He is sitting behind the hedge, hoping Mrs. Jones has left him a saucer of milk. It's all in my head.'

'Have you tried talking back?' Heli put her hand around Willow trying to ease her distress a little.

'No, don't be daft...should I?' Willow frowned.

'I'm not sure...I think we need to talk to Rose and Tammy, if you don't want to talk to Lilly.' Heli's gaze drifted over to Jacen and Sheila again.

'I agree. We should go and see Gran tomorrow.' Willow climbed to her feet and walked down to the stream, followed by Heli. She sank down on the grassy bank of the stream, removed her shoes, and nibbled on some of Jacen's chocolate bar.

As Willow sat on the bank and paddled her toes, Jacen tried to explain to Sheila why his skin was warm. 'You Humans are so weird! And your skin's not wet either!' The Sprite paused. 'Can I touch your face?' She asked Jacen.

'Erm, yeah, if you like,' Jacen replied and leaned closer.

Sheila squeezed and pulled at Jacen's face. 'So warm...and *dry,'* the Sprite said.

Willow smiled. Two red admiral butterflies landed on her forearm. 'I knew I smelled chocolate,' said Maud the butterfly, who had a slightly damaged wing.

'Well I was the one that said it was this way,' Hector, the other said, wiggling his antennae. 'Mmm...I think it has raisins...' Hector wiggled his antennae again, 'and hazelnuts.' Hector flew closer to Willow's hand. 'May we please have some?'

'Of course.' Willow broke a small piece off and placed it on her arm. She watched as the two butterflies uncurled their long tongues and tasted the chocolate.

'You know, Hector, that young sparrow nearly caught me earlier,' Maud said as she sucked the chocolate.

'I told you not to fly over that side of the field,' Hector replied around slurps of chocolate.

'Yes, well, I saw Mrs. Thomas's cat hiding in the long grass. Those sparrow babies need to watch themselves,' Maud warned.

'I see you're talking to the butterflies now. That's new.' Heli sat down beside Willow. 'Are you okay?'

'I'm finding this all too much,' Willow sighed. 'I want to be ordinary. Why aren't I normal?' Down at the stream Jacen laughed at Sheila, who, in response, squealed in delight.

'You could come and meet my family?' Sheila invited Jacen.

'Where are they?' Jacen asked, his eyes widening in amazement at the thought of a whole family of Sprites who he had never noticed.

'Oh, in the main river. I come here to talk to Norma the Tree Sprite. She lives in the big willow that Child of Nature was sitting under,'

Sheila grinned as she pointed to where Willow sat. Jacen scrunched his face up with confusion as he couldn't see anyone else other than Willow.

Heli hugged Willow. 'I haven't covered this at Guardian Elf school yet, it's happening too soon.'

'I have to understand what's happening to me,' Willow frowned. 'I need to talk to Grandma Rose; she is much more understanding than Mum.'

'Yeah, but when?' Heli chewed on a piece of grass. 'Tomorrow's Saturday.'

Willow's eyes widened, a plan formulating quickly. 'I could be back before anyone knew I was gone.' A triumphant smile lit up her face, *yes this was a good idea* she thought, her confidence returning.

'What are you saying?' Heli got to her feet, wading across the stream to where Jacen was lying on the bank. Sheila carried on talking, not noticing as he dozed in the warm sun. Eventually, he rose and walked over to Willow.

'Done talking to Sheila, then?' Willow asked.

'Yeah, I got bored. Girls – Elf, Sprite, or Human – they are all the same. Sheila kept comparing me to the boy Sprites that live in the river, telling me who was swimming with whom, like I knew them or even what she was talking about. I think I dozed off,' Jacen laughed. 'Apart from you, of course – you're not like other, what I mean is...you are you.' Jacen blushed, 'You know what I mean.'

'Oh, thanks – I think,' Willow said and tucked some hair behind her ears, careful not to dislodge the butterflies. 'Want some chocolate?' Willow broke off two large chunks and handed them to Jacen.

'Yes, please.' The two butterflies abandoned Willow and perched on Jacen's shoulder as he retrieved the pieces. Jacen leaned back on his elbows. The butterflies drifted into the air and hovered for a few seconds. Jacen brushed them away.

'Well, how rude. I thought he was going to share with us like Child of Nature,' Hector said as the two fluttered away past the stream.

'That's just the male Human, they are quite aggressive, you know.' Maud fluttered after Hector. 'No manners.'

Willow smirked; they seemed to flutter in an angry motion on their delicate wings.

'You're very quiet, Willow,' Jacen said.

'Oh sorry – I was just thinking.' Willow reclined on the grass. She set her mind for the following day. She would sneak out of the house. She had some questions as to why everyone kept referring to her as Child of Nature and Gran was the perfect person to answer them. She didn't want to hurt her mum's feelings, but she felt like she wouldn't be as truthful about all of this as Gran. One of the best things that she had found about old people was that they generally didn't have time to be tactful.

'Hey, Jacen,' said Willow pointing at the sky, 'don't you think that cloud there looks a bit like a rabbit if you shut one eye and squint a bit?'

****

Willow opened her eyes and grabbed the alarm clock, fumbling in the dark to turn it off. She felt about on her bedside table for the switch to her little reading lamp.

The soft glow broke the blanket of darkness. Willow smiled as the snores of her dad drifted from across the hall. She could see a chink of light through the curtain as she climbed out of bed. She put her clothes on, stopping briefly when a floorboard creaked, then carefully moved over to the other bed by the wall to jab Heli awake.

'What do you want?' Heli pulled her duvet up under her chin and rolled over.

'Heli, get up,' Willow whispered. 'We're leaving to see Gran.'

'Wait, you didn't say I had to come. What time is it anyway?' Heli grunted.

'About six?' said Willow as she grabbed her bag and left the room.

'Ugh, you have got to be kidding me,' Heli moaned and shoved away her duvet. 'I'm not going anywhere without some sort of breakfast.'

Downstairs, Willow put the kettle on; because their home was an old farmhouse, it had an AGA, a kind of cross between an oven and an open coal fire. She placed two slices of bread in the toaster that sat on the kitchen work top. As the kettle started to rattle, Heli trudged in with a frown and stood by the toaster waiting for it to pop, catching the toast as it flew into the air and putting it on a plate. She plopped onto a chair at the table. Pulling the butter toward her she buttered the toast before chomping into it.

'Hurry up, Heli. Dad will be up in a minute,' Willow said.

Heli glared at Willow and chewed with her mouth open.

Willow sorted out the contents of her duffel bag, checking she had her phone, wallet, and some snacks for later. 'Come on, Heli,' Willow whispered.

It was too late. William stood in the doorway, yawning. He was dressed in shorts and a t-shirt and was holding his revision books and tablet. He stared at Willow. He then turned to Heli and frowned as Heli opened a link that allowed him to hear her.

'He wants to know where you're going,' Heli said, still munching on her toast.

'Just out,' replied Willow. She rummaged through her bag and pretended to look for something.

'Out where?' William feigned a look of innocence as he put his books and tablet down.

'He wants to know where,' said Heli. 'He thinks you're hiding something, and he wants to know what.'

'Well, tell him it's none of his business.' Willow frowned.

'*And* he says you have a knack for getting him into trouble and he is bound to get blamed for whatever you're up to this time.'

'Oh, for goodness' sake,' Willow hissed and looked up from her bag. 'Tell him I am going to Gran's, if he *must* know – and he dare not tell Mum!' Willow shot a venomous glare at her stepbrother.

William stood still, thinking. Heli shoved the last bite of toast into her mouth and sat back in her chair. Her eyes darted between the siblings like a spectator at a tennis match. William turned back to Heli again.

'He says you're not allowed to go by yourself and you know that – and that it's too far to bike to from here.' William crossed his arms, convinced his logical deductions had just won him the argument.

'Well, I'm not going by bike. I was going by *tree* if he must know,' Willow smiled. 'Anyway, shouldn't he be with Dad at the greenhouse?'

'Well, in that case I will tell Mum. And no, I came down to do some revision in the office. Dad's having a lie in,' Heli passed on the words to Willow.

William strode to the kitchen table, pulled out two slices of bread from the open packet and dropped the slices into the toaster.

'What's going on?' Althea walked in and sat next to Heli. Willow sighed upon seeing the older Elf. Althea stopped smiling and narrowed her eyes at Heli. She connected with Heli's mind. 'What's all this about, Heli?'

'Willow tried to sneak off to Gran's, William caught her, he said she can't go and that he's gonna tell Lilly. Now they're arguing. You know, the usual.' Heli shrugged.

'Oh, you're going to Gran's?' Althea chirped. 'Can I come? I miss Tammy.'

'Yeah, great! Let's all go. We'll form an expedition,' Willow complained, with barely concealed annoyance.

Althea's face fell and her eyes looked bright, as if she was going to cry. She folded her arms across her chest.

'William, please!' Willow approached her brother. 'This is important. I need to speak to Gran. Please don't tell. Mum. *Please*.' Willow widened her eyes.

William threw his arms in the air and let them drop while looking at the ceiling. 'He's coming with you!' Heli and Althea chimed in unison.

CHAPTER FOUR

Even though it was early, the strong August sunshine was burning away the mist from the stream. Gentle rays warmed the bare skin on the children's arms and legs. The warm air was filled with the scent of freshly mowed grass.

William and Willow ambled down the lane from the house, unaware of the little eyes watching them. Heli and Althea held hands, chatting in their odd Elf language behind them. In every bush, tree, and shrub little creatures hid, watched, and waited.

Willow stopped by the large oak tree at the top of the lane. She turned to William who held Heli's hand. Althea was looking at a flower in the hedgerow and not really paying attention. She hummed to herself and watched Willow.

'Are you ready?' Willow asked William. William nodded, but as Willow reached out her hand to touch the gnarled bark, a swarm of tiny green beetles surrounded the base of the tree, creating a swirling green mist that crept up from the roots and surrounding vegetation.

The mist moved deliberately towards Willow's feet and purposefully wrapped itself around her legs. She shivered as a cold sweat broke out over her body. The tendrils of mist felt as if they were burning her skin, seeping into her pores, and turning her bones to ice.

Now, the mist drifted further up her body, burning, and freezing her all at once, a most curious sensation! Willow tried to move her arms, but they just hung there, limp, and unmoving.

Willow turned her head to William, her eyes large in her white face. She tried to open her mouth, but it refused to obey her. Willow cleared her mind and concentrated on Heli.

'Run, William...run now!' Willow thought with all her might, screwing her eyes shut. When she opened them all she could see was opaque green mist around her. A high-pitched buzzing reverberated in her head. Willow shook it vigorously, but the sensation didn't go away.

'Shut the link, Willow,' Heli seemed to scream in her head. Willow imagined a door closing and suddenly Heli's screaming was gone. Willow sagged and her eyes closed. Her body felt like all the world's gravity was pushing down on it. The buzzing had changed and now it seemed like she was hearing waves crashing on a beach, lulling her to sleep. All thoughts of William left her head.

'Yes,' voices whispered in her ear, 'sleep, Child of Nature, and come to us.' Willow's body relaxed and the weight lifted. Her arms and legs felt as if they were cotton wool as all the tension flowed out of her, and she drifted into a welcome sleep.

William's brow creased and his eyes widened as his body went rigid with shock. The green mist engulfed Willow so quickly – he reached out his hand to pull her away, but he lost all feeling where the mist touched his skin.

Like a living thing, which it surely appeared to be, it turned and crawled toward William and Heli. William's head filled with a muted buzzing sound and he had to focus to block it out. Then utter silence as Willow and Heli shut off their telepathic link to each other and to him.

'Althea! Run! Go get Mum!' William shouted, though he was not sure how much sense he made. It worked. Althea turned and darted down the lane back towards the house.

Focus, William thought, as his arms tingled, and his hairs stood on end. His pupils dilated. His vision sharpened. His beating heart quickened; adrenalin pumped through his body. A cold sensation crept through his feet. They dwindled into numbness as the cold slowly clawed up his legs, stinging as it touched his skin. The mist flowed like an unstoppable flood. William felt as if his legs were full of thick wet cement and his blood vessels were clogging up.

There's not much time, he thought. Then it came to him in a flash of inspiration: *the tree!*

William took a deep breath, and using all the strength he had left, forced his body forward. Unable to move his legs he toppled like a tree that had been cut from its roots. He felt his chest crash into Willow's shoulder, forcing all the air from his lungs.

As Willow's hand met the tree, a shimmering haze appeared. The bark seemed to peel back, coalescing, and revealing a light-filled door in its trunk. William grabbed Heli and pushed Willow through. As she tumbled into the tree, William fell after her, all the while clutching the little Elf.

Althea watched as the shimmering light appeared in the tree and seemed to swallow the children up as they fell forward. With tears streaming down her face, she turned and ran. In her haste she tripped and fell, grazing her cheek and knees, but she scrabbled to her feet and, ignoring the pain, continued to run. Althea burst into the kitchen.

Lilly was sitting at the kitchen table, her back to the door, facing the AGA and enjoying the peace. She turned as Althea staggered in. Startled, she knocked over her tea.

'Oh, Althea there you are! You made me jump – where have you been?' Lilly said. 'Are the children up as well? Do you want a cup of tea? You look awfully pale.'

Lilly got up to fetch a cloth from the sink to mop up the spilt tea. 'What's the matter?' Lilly moved over to the AGA and put the kettle on to boil again.

Lilly waited for Althea to catch her breath as she fetched another mug. Althea's chest was heaving. Tears welled at the corners of her eyes.

Leaves tangled in the dishevelled little Elf's hair and mud stained her jeans. Althea plucked two leaves from her hair and laid them on the table, frowning. She had grazed her cheek.

Lilly finished making the tea and brought both mugs over to the table. Slowly, Lilly sat down, putting her arm around the little Elf. She gave her a long hug and asked, 'What's going on?'

Althea shook her head and struggled to catch her breath. The stream of tears that she had been fighting back began to flow down her cheeks.

'It's the children, Miss Lilly. They've been taken,' Althea sniffed. Lilly gasped, covering her mouth with her hand as she passed Althea a tissue.

'What do you mean?' Desperation grated her voice. Althea shook her head and started sobbing again.

'Okay, Al.' Lilly put her fingers to her temples and rubbed them slowly in little circles as she tried to think. 'Start at the beginning. Tell me everything that happened this morning.'

Lilly passed Althea her tea. The Elf took a big gulp and winced at the bitter taste then she blew her nose and took a deep breath. 'Oh, Miss Lilly, Willow and William are lost. They got Heli too.'

'When you say "lost", what exactly do you mean?'

'Willow wanted to go see her Grandma Rose to talk to her about what the Sprite said to Heli yesterday. William found her and Heli in the kitchen and he and Willow had an argument. He insisted that he go with them. Then I wanted to go because I wanted to see Tammy.' Althea paused to blow her nose.

'Go on, Al,' Lilly urged, stroking Althea's hair like she used to do to the children when they were little and distressed.

'Well, we walked up the lane to the oak tree because Willow and William decided they would go by tree since it was too far to cycle to Gran's,' Althea sniffled, and tears rolled down again. 'I didn't notice anything strange as we walked up the lane – really, I didn't. We just walked and we didn't see anyone else.'

'It's okay Al – what happened at the tree?' Lilly felt her stomach roll and bile rise in her throat.

'When Willow reached her hand out to touch the tree, all these little beetle-like creatures came out of the hedges and grass and swarmed around her. They emitted this green mist that...I don't know.' The little Elf shook her head. 'Willow just stood there not moving and then this awfully loud buzzing started. We shut the link as quickly as we could, but then we couldn't communicate with William.'

Althea blew her nose some more. 'Then they turned to William and Heli and me. I could not tell William to run – not that he would have, the idiot, he always feels he must protect Willow. That is when William grabbed Heli and I think he told me to run back here. When I looked back, he pushed Willow into the tree, but Willow was unconscious, so she couldn't give the tree any instructions...so who knows where it sent them.'

Lilly ran both her hands through her hair and shut her eyes, sighing with relief. She turned back to Althea. 'Well that's not so bad,' Lilly got up and walked over to the AGA and picked up the kettle. Taking it to the sink, she refilled it with water before walking back to the stove and putting the kettle on to boil for more tea.

'We should be able to find them,' Lilly leaned against the table. 'Well, the tree would send them somewhere it considered safe,' Lilly said out loud, while thinking. *But where…? Well first I need to get dressed and then contact the office. The tree may have sent them to a member of the Elder Council.*

'But Miss Lilly, there is more. When the mist engulfed Willow there was a loud buzzing in her head, so we shut the link – but then William couldn't hear me warn him about the tree. He's so tall, when William pushed everyone into the tree, I saw him bang his head, and he seemed to go limp right before he vanished.'

Lilly gasped as she put her hand over her mouth. 'Are you sure, it wasn't just a trick of the light as he fell?' The Elf shook her head.

'What is going on, Lilly?' Althea asked. 'What were those things and why were they after the children?' Althea spooned some sugar into her mug of tea and stirred it with force before slurping it.

'Whatever they were, they knew all about Guardian Elves and the link,' Lilly mused, getting up and putting her mug in the sink.

'Was it my fault?' Althea said in a high-pitched voice. 'Should I have done more to save them?' Althea looked at Lilly with watery eyes. 'I'm a Guardian Elf and I failed.' Her little chest heaved as she gasped for breath amid uncontrollable tears. 'They could be anywhere,' she squeaked.

Lilly closed her eyes and fell back into her chair. 'You're right. The children could be anywhere in the country, or world, for that matter – and William could possibly have a serious head injury.'

'What were those things and why did they attack the children?' Althea looked at Lilly.

'You're sure the children were the intended victims?' Lilly asked, pacing the kitchen.

'Well, yes, I think so...I mean, how else would those things know about William and the link?' Althea reasoned. She had stopped crying and was now watching Lilly's thoughtful pacing.

'Maybe they didn't, maybe it was only Willow they were after...Willow and Heli.'

Lilly stopped and turned to Althea. 'Al, what if this is about me?'

Althea gasped, her eyes widening as realisation dawned. 'You think someone was trying to kidnap Willow and Heli but got William as well?'

'Yes. Why did Willow feel she couldn't confide in me? What happened that she had to go and see Grandma Rose?' Lilly started pacing again. 'Right – Althea you contact Tamarix to get Gran here. I'll get dressed and wake David up.'

The little Elf nodded, hiccupped, and disappeared out of the kitchen. There was so much to do!

CHAPTER FIVE

William could smell pine. *How weird*, he thought, as he started to register more sensations. His head ached a lot and he was lying on something prickly and uncomfortable.

Somewhere far off, a soft weeping echoed in the bleary darkness. He could hear again. The link had returned, which meant Heli must be nearby.

He could feel a breeze on his skin, and it occurred to him that he ought to open his eyes to see where he was. Thoughts skittered across his brain as he drifted back. A cutting pain dug into his head and he groaned. He could still smell pine and feel the breeze on his skin, indicating he was outside. Trying to think was like trying to swim through treacle. He felt someone holding his hand.

'William?' Far away, someone was saying his name. William tried to focus.

'Are you awake?' whispered Willow. William dragged his consciousness toward Willow's voice. He could hear fear in her voice.

'Are you alive?' Willow shook William, making him groan.

'I don't think you should shake him, Willow.' Heli sat on William's other side stroking his hand.

'He won't wake up – he should wake up,' Willow's voice struggled as she tried not to cry. 'Please, please, please wake up,' she sobbed.

'I am awake, sadly,' William coughed. He winced as Willow awkwardly hugged him. He lifted his hand and stroked her hair as she rested her head on his shoulder. William cautiously wiggled his fingers and toes, noting with relief that the only thing causing pain was his head.

'And no. I am not dead. Although, that might be an improvement from how I feel at the moment,' William managed groggily.

'Woah, did you just kiss me?'

'Yeah, I thought you were dead! And I'm so pleased you're not.' Willow held his hand.

William tried to open his eyes, but one remained glued shut. Probably blood, William decided after swallowing a bitter metallic taste in his mouth. William was right. He felt a nasty gash above his right eye. 'Where are we?' he asked.

'This looks like a managed forest,' Willow said, wiping her face. The trees in the pine forest around them aligned into rows and columns. A breeze howled through the tops of the trees. 'And it's not warm here like in Dorset. I think we are in the North – maybe Scotland? Especially with all these pines...' Willow cast her gaze around the dark forest and between the trees, hoping to spot a blue or grey patch of sky, or even some green vegetation that would lead them to the edge of the woods.

'Can you see anything?' Heli asked from where she was sitting.

'Nope, not a thing, not even a bird,' Willow replied.

All Willow could see was row upon row of pine trees, all perfectly spaced. She admired the precision of the planting. *Just my luck to end up in such a sterile environment. I bet no one ever comes here*, Willow thought.

'I think I need a doctor or something,' said William.

Willow felt about in her bag and pulled out her mobile phone, holding it up with triumphant grin – but frowned as she turned it on. 'No signal. Not a single bar,' Willow sighed.

She got up and walked over to William, then knelt down next to him. 'It's getting dark, William. I can't get you to a doctor. We are going to have to stay here tonight, sorry.' Willow took his hand and squeezed it.

'Why – why can't we use a tree?' William managed at last as even thinking hurt.

'I can't. I don't know what happened, but it doesn't work at the moment, and you're too sick to move. We should stay here for now.'

'We need to find shelter or build a fire or something.' Willow grazed her fingers along the dense bed of pine needles that smothered the forest floor. 'It will be difficult to find any ground level vegetation. Even rhododendrons won't grow here with all these needles, never mind something that I can actually use to build a shelter, like a decent bit of willow or elder.' Willow giggled, making Heli giggle.

'Yeah, very funny, Willow,' William rasped. 'How is it already going dark? How long have we been here?'

'I don't know,' she replied. 'That mist was like an anaesthetic – I just woke up.' Willow rubbed her arms. She could feel a chill in the air which she was sure wouldn't be good for William. 'I'm going to light a fire to keep us warm.'

Willow paused and looked at her brother. Heli held his hand. William was as pale as Heli's white shirt.

'Can you get up William?'

William tried to sit up. His head spun and he leaned over to be sick. Sweat broke out on his forehead.

'William, don't,' Heli soothed, easing him back down. 'Willow have you got anything in that bag to clean William up with?'

'Ugh,' William groaned. 'I haven't felt like this since I downed that bottle of vodka at Tom's party last summer.' He lay back down and closed his eyes.

Willow rummaged through her bag again. 'Here!' She tossed a packet of tissues and a small bottle of water to Heli. 'Use these to clean the blood off his face so I can see where the cut is – and how bad it is.' Willow turned to the Elf. 'Heli, don't let him go to sleep.'

The little Elf knelt next to William and, wetting the tissue, cleaned off the blood.

'William, open your eyes, please stay awake.'

'Ouch Heli, that really hurts.'

Willow returned to rummaging through her bag.

'Thanks,' said William, 'but have you got anything else in that bag for my headache?' William moaned as he eased himself upright. He held back an urge to vomit. His head felt like a herd of Jacen's cows were tap dancing on his brain.

'No, sorry,' said Willow. 'The water might help, though.' Willow sighed upon finding the box of matches she carried in her bag. She shook the box to check there were any matches left inside. *Yes!*

She had brought them when her dad had taken them camping. He had hired one of those old camper vans and taken her and William to Dartmoor; it had been fun, except their Dad could not cook and, after two days of beans on toast, they had persuaded him to stop at a pub and at that point they decided to declare the camping holiday a failure. She shoved the small cardboard box in her pocket and stood up. 'I need to find something suitable to build the fire in…'

'Just don't burn the place down,' William smirked through his pain. 'This whole area seems dry. If this is Scotland, I don't think it has seen rain very recently.' William groaned as Heli helped him over to a tree for support.

The movement reopened the gash and fresh blood dripped onto his cheek.

'Sit back,' Heli instructed as she dabbed gently with a tissue.

****

Willow returned to their little campsite with her collection of stones and sticks. She arranged the stones in a circle on the ground in front of the tree William and Heli were sitting against. She hollowed out a small trench around the stones with a stick and scraped away any pine needles surrounding the small hearth leaving nothing but bare earth.

Willow sat back and smiled at her handiwork. Perhaps Girl Guides wasn't a complete waste of time after all, she thought. Next, Willow collected dead sticks and pinecones from the ground under the surrounding trees and piled them inside her stone circle.

William sat leaning against his tree and watched. Though his wound was deep, it had stopped bleeding. A smile spread across Willow's face.

'What's so funny?' William asked. Heli started giggling.

'I was just picturing Dad's face, trying to think of a suitable punishment for me after he hears I accidently killed you,' Willow chuckled.

'That's really not funny, Willow.' William hid his smile.

Willow pulled the box of matches from her pocket and took one out. She struck it to light the fire. The sticks and pinecones were brittle and dry. Willow used the tissues with which Heli had cleaned William's face to get it going. As soon as Willow saw a tendril of smoke, she knelt low and gently blew until a small flame danced to life, licking at the dried wood. William stuck his thumbs up at Willow as he watched the flame, while Heli hugged her.

The fire seemed to take on a life of its own, casting a bright glow across their little clearing as the smoke weaved upwards and the dry wood crackled and burned.

Willow stared into the fire. She cupped her hands against the heat and sighed. 'How are they going to know where we are? How are they even going to know where to look for us?' Panic filtered through Willow's voice. 'Do you think they even know we've gone missing yet?' Heli moved to sit with Willow, putting her arm around her.

'Mum and Dad know what has happened,' William said. 'I sent Althea back to the house to tell them right before I hit my head. I expect they are probably already looking for us. Willow nodded and looked slightly less strained. Heli leaned against Willow and hugged her tighter.

'We stay here tonight and, in the morning, we reassess our situation,' Heli grinned.

They lapsed into silence before William raised his head to look at Willow. 'So why exactly do you keep a box of matches in your bag?' he asked.

'I'm not a pyromaniac or anything. They're just for emergencies,' she said.

'Oh right, you have lots of emergencies requiring matches then?' William raised a brow.

Willow laughed 'No, only when I try to tree travel with you.'

'Willow, there is no way I'm travelling by tree with you again. We'll just have to try and figure out where we are in the morning and alert the local authorities,' William said, resting his head on his arm whilst he lay back on the ground. He closed his eyes to try and banish his awful headache.

'Don't be such a baby,' Willow said. 'How else are we going to get home? Did you miss the bit about us being in Scotland? Are you hungry? I have some chocolate and an apple in my bag,' Willow said, changing the subject before William could object.

'No thanks,' he muttered sleepily.

Wow! Thought Willow, *he must be really ill if he is not even arguing*. Willow settled down next to him. The fire popped and crackled as the flames danced over the wood.

'You alright Willow?' Heli said from by her side.

'Yeah. You okay, Heli?' the little Elf nodded but did not speak any more as she got up and lay down next to William.

Willow felt warm at last and lay down on the ground. She wrapped her arms around her brother, snuggled close to keep him safe, and closed her eyes.

★★★★

David entered the kitchen to find Lilly and Althea deep in conversation at the table. They were speaking the odd Elf language he did not know; David wished he had paid attention in his grammar school Latin class.

'Good morning you two,' David said, turning to Lilly. 'I thought you'd be at the supermarket buying half the snack aisle as you usually are for William and Willow,' he laughed.

David touched the kettle on the AGA. He decided it was hot enough and brewed a coffee.

'What's going on?' David asked as he took his coffee and sat at the table opposite Lilly. 'What is so important that I had to get up this early?' he asked Lilly and the Elf.

'David, there has been an incident involving the children,' started Lilly.

'What sort of incident?' David stopped what he was doing and tensed. He gazed at Lilly first and then Althea. 'Please could someone explain to me what sort of trouble a fifteen-year-old and a nineteen-year-old can get into this early on a Saturday morning?'

Before Lilly could answer, Grandma Rose swept in, closely followed by her Elf, Tamarix.

'Gran!' Lilly jumped to her feet and hugged Rose. 'Thank goodness you're here. Someone tried to kidnap the children and now they are lost, and William's hurt, and I am not entirely sure what to do,' Lilly blurted out in one breath.

'What!' David fumed. 'Why haven't you contacted the police?' David ran his hands through his hair and gulped his coffee.

'It's more complicated than that,' Lilly said. 'We can't tell anyone, at least not yet.' Lilly looked at David. 'Please David, I know I'm asking a lot of you, but I need you to trust me on this.'

Lilly walked around the table and drew a chair next to him. She clutched his hand in hers. 'You've always been so understanding.' Lilly gazed at David's face. 'I couldn't ask for a more patient and loving husband even when I told you who I was...' Lilly looked into his blue eyes. 'But you still stuck by me. Please David we can't tell anyone.'

'Ok...' David said after a long pause. 'But why in heaven's name not? Just explain to me what you think is going on!'

'Because...' Lilly fell silent.

'Because,' Gran said, 'You suspect Elf involvement, don't you Lilly?'

Lilly nodded. 'Yes Gran. I'm afraid I do.' Lilly smiled weakly at David.

'So, what does your gut instinct tell you to do, Lilly?' Gran enquired as she picked up the kettle and carried it to the sink.

'My instinct's telling me not to trust anyone,' Lilly said. 'Because whoever is behind this knows us. They also know that Willow is starting to acquire and use her powers and that she can travel by tree. So, whoever is involved is either someone from the Elf world – or that someone in FERA is acting as a mole and selling secrets to the Dark Elves,' Lilly said.

'What about William? Did they know he was going to be there?' David looked at Lilly.

'No, I think that was bad luck.'

'So, you're saying someone planned to take Willow, and William got in the way.' David gulped his coffee.

'Do we have any idea why she was coming to see me?' Grandma Rose interrupted.

'No not really, I didn't get a chance to talk to Heli last night. Heli did say that Willow was addressed by her title yesterday,' Althea answered from where she was now sitting with Tammy.

'This all suggests this is targeted at you Lilly, if it was only Willow, they were after. Suggesting they know she is Child of Nature,' Grandma Rose concluded.

'How though? We never address her as that.' Lilly put her head in her hands, her eyes wide with shock.

'Well, that can only mean it is someone who knows who you really are.' David pulled Lilly onto his lap and wrapped his arms around her.

'I thought we had been careful keeping her away from that world, keeping her safe.' Lilly buried her head in David's neck.

'I know you did sweetheart,' David said.

'Whoever they are, I doubt they will want a monetary ransom,' Grandma Rose said.

'I need to speak to Lord Hurleston then,' Lilly mumbled.

'Yes, but I suggest we wait,' Grandma Rose answered.

'What, why are you waiting,' David demanded.

'Because it hasn't been long enough. Willow is resourceful. She could walk back through the door any minute – it has only been a couple of hours since they went missing. Lord Hurleston or the Elder Council wouldn't do anything yet, nor would the police,' Tammy explained.

****

David trudged down the path to the elegant Victorian greenhouses that made up the garden centre. They were located just to the side of the house.

David and William spent most of their time down here. David noticed a crunching under his feet. When he looked down, he was amazed to see lots of little green and blue beetles covering the ground.

Some had started to crawl up his leg. He slipped his hand into the pocket of his trousers and pulled out a small specimen jar, which he carried for just such an occasion. He smiled. He had got into this habit while at university despite Simon's constant jokes. He missed William's father.

'Oh, William,' David whispered to himself, an air of melancholy settling in him, remembering the conversations he often had with Simon. 'Who's crazy now for carrying around a specimen jar?'

David sighed while undoing the lid of the little jar. He bent down and used the lid to scoop up some of the scuttling beetles, making sure not to touch them with his skin. He watched the beetles slide to the bottom of the glass. He then screwed the lid on tightly and placed the jar back into his pocket.

CHAPTER SIX

'Not now Heli, I'm tired,' Willow mumbled, waving a limp hand over her shoulder, and attempting to roll over.

Heli continued tapping her. 'Please, Willow. Wake up now.' Urgency laced Heli's words. Willow opened her eyes and looked around.

'What is it Heli?'

'We're not alone,' Heli whispered. Her chest heaved. 'Somebody is spying on us.'

'Where?' Willow asked and glanced around. 'Heli, I don't see anyone.'

'They are in the trees,' Heli said and gulped. 'I think...they're Dark Elves.'

'Seriously?' Willow asked, crossing her arms across her chest 'It's completely deserted here.'

'They're the ones that don't like Humans,' Heli hissed, peering around, clutching Willow's arm. 'They are the ones that cause the trouble and kill people like William's parents.'

'How do you know about William's parents?' Willow frowned.

'That's not important. They will kill us if they find us. They hate the Elder Council and especially dislike Mother Nature.' Heli shuddered.

'Hello?' Willow called out. 'Who's there? Come out in the open.'

'Willow!' Heli hissed. 'What are you doing?'

'If you are a Dark Elf, we're not scared of you!' Willow shouted, hoping she sounded more confident than she felt.

'Willow did you miss the bit about killing us,' Heli squeaked.

'No, but I'm not letting some Dark Elf kill me without putting up a fight,' Willow declared, picking up a large stick and holding it out like a sword.

Willow slowly turned in a circle. All around her, halfway up the trees, she could see sets of glowing yellow eyes. 'They are everywhere Heli.'

'Yes, I can see that. We are going to die,' Heli wailed, still clinging to Willow's arm. 'I suppose it's too late to get William and hide?'

'Well yeah, if there are Dark Elves everywhere,' Willow muttered.

'How insulting! We aren't Dark Elves, we aren't even Elves lassie. We are Tree Sprites – and you are trespassing in our woods,' a voice burred in a thick Scottish accent said.

Willow watched the Sprites peel away from the trees and dexterously climb down. Nearly twenty, three-foot-tall creatures with rough, bark-like skin and pine needles for hair, clung to the pine trees with sharp fingers and toes. Their deep-set dark eyes peered down at Willow.

Willow swallowed and stood straight, trying to appear calm. 'We just need directions,' she said. 'You see, we are a bit lost and wouldn't be here if we knew where to go.' Willow hoped the Tree Sprites would understand.

'No, we cannae give you directions, lassie,' said the Sprite. He seemed bigger than the others and braver. 'No one lives round here.'

'What about the castle, Hamish?' piped another Tree Sprite. This one was a lot smaller, and Willow wasn't sure why, but she thought it might be a girl.

'Shut it, Morag!' Hamish ordered, glaring at the little Tree Sprite, before returning his attention to Willow. 'No, there ain't anyone round here for miles and miles.'

'Wait!' Willow put her hand out as she looked at them. 'She mentioned a castle...'

'Who, her?' Hamish motioned towards Morag. 'Nah, ignore her, girly. She's a little bit slow, there isn't a castle belonging to no Winter Elves around here,' he replied with an air of surety.

'Please,' Willow begged. 'My brother William is hurt, and he needs a doctor. You have to take us to the castle.' Hamish looked at the others who all shrugged in unison.

'Aaah okay,' he said. 'If you insist...but it wasn't my idea if things don't turn out right.' He turned with the others and began to jump through the trees. Willow stood alone as she watched them go.

'What's that supposed to mean?' Willow said. 'Wait, I need help with my brother! He's hit his head and I don't think he's fit to walk!' Willow knelt beside William and shook his shoulders to wake him up. She then remembered how people with head injuries should not sleep deeply. You had to wake them up periodically and make them talk. *I hope he's fine!*

'Okay,' said Hamish. 'You four take his arms and legs and carry him.' Hamish motioned to four others. They were so well camouflaged, that Willow could barely make them out. The four looked at each other and reluctantly crawled down the pine trees to the forest floor. They seemed to creak as they moved, like tree branches blowing in the wind. Between them they managed to hoist William up above their shoulders, as though they were bearing a coffin.

'Right, you four sure you have hold of the boy,' Hamish demanded.

'Alistair, don't you drop his head,' Hamish warned.

'Yeah, yeah I know what I'm doing,' the one called Alistair that was currently holding William's head answered.

'Okay boys are you ready,' Alistair asked.

'Move it you lot, we don't have all day!' Hamish barked.

The Tree Sprites moved at a surprising speed on their short and spindly legs. Some scurried along the ground while some leapt from tree to tree.

Willow quickly stomped out the fire and grabbed her bag. She jogged to keep up with the Sprites as they moved effortlessly, balancing William on their shoulders. Heli panted as she sprinted behind Willow, trying to keep from falling too far behind.

Soon, Willow started to notice that the trees were getting further apart and that it was now a lot brighter. The sun's rays streaked through the canopy of trees.

Willow glanced upwards as she jogged along, and, in the distance, she could see turrets with flags fluttering in the breeze. Then, not long after, she could see the entire façade of an imposing Scottish castle. She felt the hairs on the back of her neck raise.

'Right, this is as far as we go,' the Sprite leader said. 'You'll have to manage him from here.'

The four Sprites dumped William on the grass like a sack of spuds, no haggis-deference given. Willow rushed to him and checked for his pulse. William was still okay.

'Okay and thank you Sprites!' Willow said. 'We were in some real trouble back there,' Willow called as she tried to pick up William.

'Goodbye, Child of Nature,' they chorused and soon disappeared into the woods. Willow felt lost and alone again.

'Grab his arm Heli we need to get him on his feet,' Willow instructed.

'Ugh he is way too heavy; he owes me for this!' Heli grumbled as she hoisted William's arm around her shoulders.

'We're heading to the front of the castle,' Willow advised as she tugged William's sleeping body towards a large set of oak doors in the middle of the castle's three-level façade. A pair of tall, cylindrical towers topped with black-slated conical roofs flanked either side of the entrance. Looming behind the towers stood the much older keep, the central and original part of the castle, which sported battlements and a flagpole with a white flag fluttering on top of it.

The flag featured an intricate coat of arms composed of a red, white, and orange shield with five snowflakes in relief. Two vicious dragons flanked the shield. Antlers protruded from their heads instead of horns. *They look more deer than lizard!* Willow thought. *Save for the fact they have featherless wings and breathe fire.*

Above the shield and dragons was a helmet from a medieval suit of armour. A long plume of feathers sprouted from the helmet, in the same red, yellow, and white colours as the shield.

'I really hope someone's in,' Willow muttered as she struggled towards the front doors. Then, the large oak doors opened magnificently, and a group of ten or eleven people in black and white office clothes rushed towards them.

'Oh, you poor children. Here let us help,' a smartly dressed, slightly plump middle-aged Scottish woman said as she rushed forward to grab William. 'You poor things come with us, have you eaten?' another lady asked.

'What happened to you?' one of the men asked. 'Would you like us to call someone?'

One man stood out from the group.

He had short, neat, bone-white hair and wore a green tweed three-piece suit. He was standing away from the group and looked to be in his late thirties to early forties. The man smiled, showing off an even set of pearly white teeth. As he approached, Willow noticed his deep, dark-blue eyes and found that, although his people (as by his bearing he had to be in charge) were all around fussing over her, she could barely take her eyes off him. He was strangely captivating.

'Here dear, let us see to the young man,' a thin beaky-looking woman addressed Willow. Two men in natty suits picked William up and carefully carried him into the castle.

★★★★

Taranis flashed a triumphant smile as he walked down the stone steps towards the two girls.

As he approached the lawn where they stood, he glanced at the unconscious boy his staff carried past him and into the castle. Taranis turned his attention to the girls. Willow smiled nervously, knotting her hands behind her back, as he focused his violet blue eyes on her.

'Goodness a Guardian Elf. You must be very important my dear,' he smiled.

'Um no, not really,' Willow mumbled, feeling her cheeks heat up.

'She is Child of Nature, and if you recognise a Guardian Elf you will know to show her due respect.' Heli scowled.

'Of course,' he flicked his eyes over Heli as if to dismiss her. Heli glared at him from under her lashes, her mouth set in a line. *Jeez Winter Elves are so snotty*, Heli scowled.

'My dear child look at you,' Taranis said, surreptitiously moving between Willow and Heli, and placing his hand on Willow's back, guiding her forward. 'Come inside where it's warm and we'll see about fixing you something nice to eat. You look as though you haven't slept in days.'

'Thank you that would be great!' Willow glared at Heli who poked her tongue out, showing her displeasure.

'My name is Taranis. It's an ancient family name, and luckily for you both, I also happen to be the King of the Winter Elves,' Taranis said. 'Your Elf was very clever leading you here.' Taranis smiled at Heli, who stopped scowling and grudgingly smiled hearing the compliment.

'It's nice to meet you, sir. My name is Willow,' Willow said. 'And this is my Elf, Heli.' Willow spoke with a hint of hesitation as she gazed at him.

She shivered involuntarily as she surveyed his handsome face. Willow glanced at Heli who smiled back and squeezed her hand tight. Willow felt the muscles in her stomach clench with unease. 'I don't trust him,' Willow thought.

'Neither do I,' Heli responded telepathically.

'And the unconscious boy, who is he?' Taranis asked.

'His name is William. He's my brother,' Willow said. 'Where have you taken him?'

'Don't worry, my dear,' Taranis said. 'He's just been taken to the state room where a medic can take a look at that nasty cut on his head.' He paused before speaking again. 'Now this may sound odd, but you do not happen to be Lilly Millbank's children, do you?' Taranis asked. 'William looked awfully familiar.'

'Yes, yes we are,' Willow said, a smile touching the corners of her mouth. 'Do you know her? What luck!' Willow said as her shoulders relaxed. She beamed at Heli.

'Well yes,' Taranis said. 'Being the King of Winter, I work with her all the time.' Taranis gestured to a kind-looking lady with the same white hair as Taranis. 'Now why don't you go with Marie here and she'll prepare some soup and sandwiches. Maybe even hot chocolate if you're lucky!'

Marie smiled at Willow and Heli. 'I will phone your mother and tell her that you're all alright. She must be worried sick, I'm sure.' Taranis flashed another smile.

Marie led Willow and Heli through the winding corridors towards the direction of the kitchen and the promise of a good, hearty meal.

Taranis, meanwhile, strolled through the long, ancient hallways to his study. He sat down at his large oak desk and poured himself a scotch.

The abduction went remarkably well, he thought to himself, as he leaned back in his chair, his hands behind his head.

CHAPTER SEVEN

William woke up to find himself tucked under a plush down comforter, on a spongy four poster bed. Willow was sitting by the bed, in an old-fashioned chair, her legs dangling over the armrest. 'Feeling better?' she asked.

'Where are we?' William pushed himself up. He noticed his head did not ache as much and that he didn't feel sick.

'Scotland – I was right,' Willow said. 'We are in King Taranis' castle – he's the king of the Winter Elves. He says we will be safe here until our parents can come and get us.'

'How did we get here?' William asked. 'When I went to sleep, we were in some wood.' William looked around the lavish room. Wood panels furnished the walls and a chandelier dangled from a high ceiling adorned with decorative plaster work. At the opposite end, wooden columns supported the mantel-piece of a mammoth marble fireplace.

'Oh, you know,' Willow said. 'I met some cool Sprites. I asked them for help. They brought us here.'

'Then why do you still look worried, Willow? And where's Heli?'

'She's hiding in the corner,' Willow said. Heli giggled. She walked over to the bed and climbed up next to William.

'I don't like it here William. I want to go home.' Heli said, taking his hand.

'I don't like it here either,' Willow said. She swung her legs round and gazed at him with her large stormy grey eyes.

'Why? Surely we are safe here?' William felt confused. 'What is bothering you, Willow? This is a vast improvement from being stuck in a pine forest!'

'I don't know,' said Willow, as she got out of her chair and sat on William's bed. 'I think someone was trying to kidnap us – and whoever was behind it knew all about us, including the fact that you're linked to the Guardian Elves. They don't normally interact with other Humans. They just have one Human. So, what Althea and Heli do with you is well...unusual. Only we know about the Elves and you.'

Willow looked into William's dark emerald-green eyes. 'Look, I'm really relieved that you're going to be alright, but I am certain that we aren't out of danger yet. Besides, I don't like King Winter. There was something off about him.'

William frowned and rubbed his eyes, 'I was puzzled as to why they forced you and Heli to shut the link with that noise, and did they do it because of me, and, if so, how did they know we were together? How did they know you were going to go to Gran's? Nothing makes any sense – and why kidnap us? What would they gain?' William ran his hands through his messy hair and noticed that the cut on his head was now plastered.

'I don't think they did. I gave that some thought while you were sleeping. I think they just got lucky. I think I was the target and you just got in the way,' Willow explained.

'Okay, what if you're right? That still doesn't explain why anyone would want to kidnap you.'

'Because William, weird stuff has been happening to me lately, that's why I was going to Gran's to ask her about it. And of course, I am the Child of Nature. How many people do you know who have a Guardian Elf?'

'What weird stuff?'

'Voices in my head and stuff. That's not important William.' Willow sighed and closed her eyes, trying to think.

'What are you talking about Willow? Of course, it is important, I mean come on think about it, what sets us apart from normal people, it is not like Mum and Dad are millionaires or anything, so what does make them special? Dad's just a research botanist, nobody cares about him but mum's flipping Mother Nature, she controls the weather and stuff,' William said, getting slightly excited.

'Don't be daft, she doesn't control the weather, she oversees the seasons or something...I think,' Willow replied.

'Are you kidding neither of you know what your mother does? She's Mother Nature, leader of the Elder Council, Protector of the wilds and Regent of the Five Elven Houses. She alone is one of the most powerful beings on the planet, with the ability to manipulate the weather to her will and is in possession of the combined powers of the Elder Council. Furthermore, as her first born daughter you will one day inherit her role.' Heli gazed at Willow.

'Hah, see William, I am special,' Willow playfully pushed her brother in the shoulder.

'Who else knows?' William looked at Heli, his expression grim.

'Not many. Your dad of course, and the Elder Council and FERA, the government organisation she works for. That's about it really.'

'Well, there you have it then, King Taranis is probably on the phone to Mum now telling her all about how we showed up at his castle out of nowhere. Mum is probably on the way to pick us up now!' William replied triumphantly.

'As great as that all is Will, I still don't know how we ended up here and intend to get to the bottom of it. I have to know what's going on,' Willow replied impatiently.

'We don't know that we were brought here. I maintain that this could still just be a massive coincidence...not everything is some evil plot or conspiracy,' William insisted, raising his voice slightly. For a moment, the pair of them were silent, both knowing that they were at an impasse.

William gingerly got off the bed and looked for his shoes, which were skilfully placed just beneath. As he bent down to pick them up a wave of dizziness washed over him, and he felt the room spinning. He put his hands on the bed to steady himself until the dizziness passed.

'What are you doing?' Willow picked up the shoes, helped William put them on and did up his laces. 'You still look really pale. Perhaps you should not be out of bed just yet,' she said.

'I want to go home. You want to go home – so what's stopping us?' William shuffled over to the door and tried the handle gently. The door opened. *Of course, it would*, he thought to himself, *why would it be locked?* 'See guests, not prisoners,' he remarked, pulling the door open further.

William poked his head out into the hallway. It was empty. He was about to call Willow when he felt her hand on his shoulder.

'Heli, do you remember which way we came?' Willow asked as they crept down the corridor. No one was around.

'No not really, and that woman Maria took us to the kitchen first,' Heli whispered.

'Well, I don't know. I was asleep,' William grinned. They walked past a couple of empty rooms, which looked like they were being used as offices, and a kitchen.

'This looks familiar,' Willow reached out and turned the door handle. The door led onto a paved terrace that overlooked a vast manicured lawn and flowerbeds. 'Wow, nice garden,' William grinned.

'Never mind the garden, look for a tree. We can use it to go home,' Willow sighed.

'It will have to be the ones in the forest. The ones in the garden are all ornamental and small,' Heli pointed out.

At the edge of the lawn, stretching over the surrounding hills like some great brown and green blanket, stood the pine forest.

'We need a big one,' Willow whispered, looking out at the wood. 'At least a hundred years old.'

'How about that one?' William pointed to a large spruce whose straight trunk soared skyward a few steps beyond the tree line.

'Yeah, that should do it,' Willow smiled and reached for his hand. Heli took his other hand, and very calmly, they walked across the lawn and into the woods towards the tree they had selected. They took each step, half-expecting to be called back, but no voice was heard, and none raised.

'Ready?' Willow enquired as she reached out her hand to touch the tree.

'Oh, I hate doing this,' William moaned. William leaned on Willow as a wave of dizziness washed over him and he felt decidedly unwell. 'Willow, wait a moment, I feel terrible.'

Willow looked at William. He had gone very pale.

'You okay William?' she asked, wrapping her arm around him.

'Yeah, just moved too quick,' he managed to say, as the urge to throw up seemed to pass. He stood up straight and Willow pressed her palm against the tree trunk causing a gateway of shimmering golden light to form in the bark.

With barely a look back the three of them passed through it and found themselves stepping out of the large willow tree just up the lane from their house.

★★★★

The children entered the kitchen to find Lilly preparing to leave.

'Mum!' Willow and William ran to Lilly and hugged her. Heli followed them, pulling out a chair and slumping down onto it.

'There you are! Where have you been?' Lilly squealed. 'I was worried sick! Queen Winter phoned to tell me you were in Scotland – I was just getting ready to go!'

'We *were* in Scotland! We tried to travel to Gran's by tree, but then we got attacked by this green mist and it made me fall asleep, so I couldn't tell the tree where to take us, and then William hit his head,' said Willow.

'Yeah – I hit my head and knocked myself out.' William pushed away his hair so Lilly could see the plaster.

'Anyway,' continued Willow, sitting next to him, 'we ended up at King and Queen Winter's castle. And when William woke up this morning, we came home.' Willow paused and looked at William.

'Good grief! That is dreadful,' Lilly said, still trying to take in everything the children had told her, her brow creasing in concern as she peered at William closely.

Lilly sat down next to him. 'Let me look at that cut,' she said, gently brushing his hair to one side. 'Do you feel alright sweetheart?'

'Yes, Mum, a little tired and a bit dizzy if I get up too quickly, but otherwise fine,' William smiled.

'Good. I had better still go to the castle and thank Taranis and Solstice in person,' Lilly smiled at the children. 'William, I think you need to go back to bed for a couple of hours and you girls need a bath and change of clothes. I won't be long. Your dad is down in his office and I will be back by dinner time,' Lilly instructed, as she reached for her handbag. She smiled at them one more time and then she and Althea left for the castle.

William looked at Willow 'Why didn't you tell her what you really suspect?' he raised a brow and settled his green eyes on her.

'Oh, if you two are going to fight, I'm going for a bath.' Heli pushed her chair out and climbed to her feet before shuffling out of the kitchen and heading for the stairs.

'Because we don't know anything did happen. Because you were right and we need to get some sort of proof as to what Taranis is up to, if he is,' Willow explained.

'How are you going to do that?'

'I thought I might just pop back, have a look round.' Willow shrugged hoping that her gesture looked casual.

'That's really dangerous Willow. You can't just break into someone's castle and snoop around,' William objected, as he glared at his sister. 'Oh, you have a plan don't you,' he sighed folding his arms on the table, and resting his forehead on them.

'Yes, I do, and I'm not going to snoop around. I am going to have a little look at his computer.'

'Why? Why do you have to go there, why can't you do it from here remotely,' William asked, lifting his head as the door opened and Jacen walked in.

'Because I can't gain access remotely, I have already tried,' Jacen said, nodding at Willow.

'What, how?' stuttered William, as Jacen pulled out a chair and sat down next to him.

'I texted Jacen from Scotland, when you were asleep and got him started on it, even before Heli told us who Mum is. I was suspicious, and kind of thought it wouldn't hurt to have a look, even if he were innocent. He seemed incredibly pleased to see us kids just show up, which is a bit odd, for a king,' Willow smiled.

Jacen looked at them both. They looked a bit grubby, and William had a large bruise on his head. 'So, are you going to fill me in properly as to where you guys have been? That text you sent was vague to say the least,' Jacen looked around, 'and where's Heli?'

'In the bath,' William said, rolling his eyes.

'Well, the thing is...yesterday, someone tried to kidnap me and William,' Willow said.

'What!' Jacen looked shocked.

'It didn't work, but William got hurt and we ended up at this castle. Only I think, sort of...' Willow shrugged. 'I think we were meant to end up there all along. That is what the green things were for. They were meant to incapacitate us and instruct the tree.' Willow rubbed her face with her hand while she thought about it.

'Whoa, what green things?' Jacen frowned.

'Never mind that. I want to have a look on a computer at the castle,' Willow spilled her words out.

'Why would anyone want to kidnap you?' Jacen frowned.

'Lots of people apparently, because of who our Mum is,' William muttered. 'Jacen, is there any way you can get on that computer from here?' William asked again.

'No, William, I explained that already. It's not as easy as people think,' Jacen sighed.

'But you can hack into just about anywhere. I mean look at the trouble you got into last year when you hacked the Pentagon,' William spluttered. 'And you can't get into a private computer?'

'Yeah, that seems to be the crux of the problem,' Jacen grinned. 'Besides, everyone does the Pentagon. It's like a rite of passage for hackers,' Jacen shrugged. 'I can only remotely access the computer if I install a programme onto it in the first place. And I have to do that physically.'

'Even if we found Taranis' computer, we don't know any of his passwords, we'd never get into it,' William reasoned.

'Oh, that bit is easy,' Jacen grinned 'Most people aren't that creative when it comes to passwords. It's probably snowball!'

'You still haven't said why we need to do this Willow. And you are potentially risking Jacen's life here,' William objected.

'Oh William. Don't be so dramatic.' Willow sighed and rolled her eyes. 'Because you know what adults are like. They will pretend nothing really happened to us, and Taranis will bluff his way out of what he has done, if he has done anything, make out he saved us, and no one will bother to ask questions. I think he could be guilty and planning something, nothing adds up. Mum is there now, I bet they are drinking tea and being ever so nice,' Willow said, flashing a mischievous smile.

'I hate to say this, but I think Willow is sort of right,' Jacen said reluctantly. 'No one will investigate what happened to you, especially if some

Scottish king came to the so-called rescue. It will just be swept under the rug and deemed a silly misadventure, that's how power operates,' he added.

'So, when are you going?' William enquired, as he knew there was nothing he could say to deter his sister.

'Tomorrow, early!' Willow and Jacen answered together. *They have a symmetry thing going on*, he thought.

★★★★

Lilly stepped out of the tree and walked towards the imposing Scottish castle where recently her children had been 'guests'.

'What do you think really went on? Willow was hiding something.' Lilly's mouth set in a hard line and her brow creased in a frown.

'I don't know, but even William was hiding something. I can usually read him easily,' Althea confessed.

'Well, we had better see what Taranis has to say for himself before we tackle the children again,' Lilly stated as she climbed the steps to the front of the castle.

Just as Lilly raised her hand to knock, the door opened, and Taranis stepped out smiling.

He was impeccably dressed as usual, wearing a tweed, green-chequered woollen suit. His white hair was perfectly combed and highlighted his violet blue eyes and perfectly proportioned features. He was more handsome than a movie star.

'Mother Nature, what a pleasure,' he said smoothly. He ushered them inside. Lilly glanced at Althea, raising a brow as she followed.

'Please King Taranis, just call me Lilly,' Lilly smiled up at him. He was a good couple of inches taller than her.

'Yes of course, Lilly,' he smiled back. 'And just call me Taranis, I don't really bother with the king bit.'

He showed them into a small, cosy sitting room. A fire blazed in the grate. Lilly walked over to a brocade-covered navy couch and sat down, Althea beside her. The room was simple and tastefully made up.

'May I get you anything?' Taranis asked politely, hovering in the doorway.

'No thank you, Taranis.'

Taranis crossed the room and sat in a wing-backed armchair opposite Lilly and waited expectantly.

'I would like to thank you for taking care of my children; it was exceedingly kind of you,' Lilly smiled.

'Mother Nature, I mean Lilly, it was my pleasure and the least I could do in the circumstances. How did they manage to get here in the first place?' he enquired, his tone smooth and polite.

'Oh, Willow is an impetuous, impulsive child and was experimenting with her gifts. Unfortunately, William got hurt trying to help her. They are awfully close,' Lilly explained, smiling.

'Teenagers can be such a handful,' Taranis said, feigning sympathy. This was all going remarkably well. Maybe Hyperion was right about how easy it would be to manipulate this Mother Nature. 'If I can be of any further assistance to you, please don't hesitate to ask,' he smiled.

'Thank you, Taranis,' Lilly rose to her feet. 'Please give my regards to Solstice, it was so kind she called me. I must get back to the children, no telling what they will get up to if left too long.'

'Indeed, who knows where they may tree to next,' Taranis murmured as he politely showed Lilly out. 'Bye, bye now!' and he waved, a bit absurdly, but it appealed to him to play the handsome host with the most.

Lilly walked across the lawn. 'What did you think?' she asked Althea.

'He was his normal impeccably smooth self. Taranis has always come across aloof, arrogant, and self-satisfied, a bit like the Winter Elves in general. Of course, not as arrogant as the Summer Elves,' Althea mused.

'Oh, but aren't you a Summer Elf?' Lilly frowned as she reached out her hand to touch the tree she had selected for the journey.

As it connected, the bark of the tree appeared to peel itself away revealing a shimmering golden door of light through which they both stepped.

'I am a Guardian Elf. Even though I was born a Summer Elf, I no longer affiliate to any of the Elf Houses, and I answer to you not the Elder Council,' Althea reaffirmed, as they walked down the lane to the house.

'Elf society is extremely complicated,' Lilly answered, a wry smile touching her lips.

CHAPTER EIGHT

Willow stood against the large tree that she was going to use to get to the castle, trying to catch her breath. She had sprinted up the lane away from the house.

That boy is always late, Willow thought just as Jacen came into sight, peddling furiously up the steep hill. Upon reaching the spot, Jacen flung his bike into the bushes and scrambled over the gate.

'Sorry I'm late! Had the devil's own job getting out of the house without those flipping twins asking questions,' he panted and wheezed to get his breath back. 'Hate that blooming hill. Remind me again why we always have to meet up here?'

'Because it's the most private place around. Where else could we meet without everyone snooping about our business?'

'You have a point there,' Jacen looked in a broad sweep. 'And where's William?'

Willow hugged Jacen. 'He's still too sick and is staying at home with Heli. Did you bring what I asked for?'

'Yeah – here,' Jacen said. After rummaging through his pockets, he produced a small flash drive.

'Mum nearly caught me, but I managed to sneak it out.' Jacen handed the device to Willow.

'Brilliant! Thanks, Jacen!' Willow put the flash drive in her pocket.

'Jacen, did you tell your mum how long you would be? Or where you were going?'

'Nope…why?' Jacen said.

'Well, if I show you something, you won't think me a bit…well, you know, weird?' Willow stuttered.

'Willow, I've spoken to a Sprite. After that, nothing you show me will be weird,' Jacen laughed. 'Come on, what's going on?' Jacen reached out and squeezed Willow's hand, giving her a goofy grin.

'Well, the thing is,' Willow sighed. 'What I left out was that the castle, in Scotland, well, the quickest way to get there is…by tree. That's the weird bit.' Willow winced as she tried to gauge his response. Jacen's brow furrowed. He stared at her in silence, trying to decide whether she was joking.

'Ok, show me,' he said eventually, trying to appear cool and detached. Willow took his hand and stepped back from the birch she had been leaning against.

'Ready?' she asked as she reached out her hand and placed her palm against the bark. As her fingers contacted the wood, a bright golden light spread out from the tree beneath her palm until you could no longer make it out against the light. Jacen stared from the tree to Willow and back to the tree, his eyes rapidly blinking.

'Okay, you are officially the coolest and weirdest person I know,' Jacen gazed at the tree and Willow.

Willow concentrated on thinking about their location: The Winter Castle. As she did, the golden light grew, spreading to envelope them both.

Jacen fought the urge to jerk his hand away from Willow's as the warm shimmering light spread around them. The instant it had covered them completely, it vanished, and Jacen found himself standing in a forest he did not recognise.

'Wow, Willow! That was not weird! That was the coolest thing ever…you can basically teleport. When did you learn to do that?' Jacen exclaimed as he staggered away from the tree.

He turned and stared at the tree, trying to make out if it was special in any way. He walked all the way round it and even put his head against it to listen for any unusual sounds.

'Um…just recently, I guess,' Willow said as she watched him examine the tree.

'I knew your family was not ordinary! Can you do anything else?' he asked, still looking at the tree.

Willow laughed. 'We *are* ordinary – lots of people can travel by tree, they just don't advertise it. Imagine the chaos if they did.'

'Okay…' scoffed Jacen. 'Coming from a person who also thinks having an Elf is normal when everyone else has dogs. Dogs are normal, cars are normal. Elves and tree travel is definitely not normal!' Jacen laughed.

The two children ambled through the wood. When they finally reached the clearing before the castle, Willow stopped Jacen from going any further.

Nudging him, she pointed over to their left where two security guards strolled along the perimeter of the castle. 'There's was no way we can sneak back in the same way we snuck out before,' Willow whispered. 'Unless we can create a diversion…'

'Ah lassie,' came a thick but familiar Scottish accent from a nearby tree. 'I see you're trespassing in our woods again – and you brought another friend.'

Willow squinted, looking above and around her, until her eyes adjusted to the camouflaged Tree Sprites clinging to their trees.

'Oh, hello,' Willow said. 'Yes, I'm afraid I am trespassing again. But you see, it is only temporary until I get back into the castle. We need to get in without being seen this time, instead of being invited guests, and there seem to be a lot of security guards about.' Willow paused. 'Can you help us?'

Hamish The Sprite in charge climbed down from the tree, followed swiftly by the others. 'We only just finished helping you from that other time, you need to try and stay out of trouble lassie.'

'Please help us. We're desperate,' Willow begged.

'Aye! Sure, we can – can't we boys?' The other Sprites nodded in agreement.

'Willow,' Jacen whispered. 'Who are these guys – and why would they want to help us?' Jacen looked at the Sprites in undisguised awe.

'Actually, that is a good question, why are you so keen to help us?' Willow asked, before adding very quickly, 'Not that we're not grateful because we are, but what's in it for you?'

'Well first, that lot in that castle have been, let's say, annoying us of late, what with all their traipsing around our woodlands and shooting pheasants. And second, we sort of well...' he looked down at his feet as if embarrassed, 'Well, we sort of have to do what you say – you being Child of Nature and all.'

'Oh, thanks. I think, it's truly kind of you Mister err...'

'You can call me Hamish, Child of Nature.'

'Well thank you for all your help Hamish, we won't forget this,' Willow replied solemnly.

'Now what sort of distraction did you have in mind Mister Sprite?' Jacen asked politely, not knowing whether he should call him Hamish as well.

'We have this little trick we have been practising with the local wildlife,' said Hamish. 'I think you're going to like it.' As Hamish said this, some of the others laughed in their odd, creaky, rustling voices.

'How will we know when you've done it?' asked Willow, her question only causing the creaky rustling laughter to intensify.

'Oh, you will know, lassie, don't you worry. Now go and stand over by the edge of the forest and get ready to run.' Willow and Jacen did as they were told.

****

King Hyperion arrived at the castle and strode at pace across the beautiful gravel drive. Four wolf-like creatures were at his heel. The Maera stopped suddenly, and they began to sniff the air and ground, snarling and baring their long razor-sharp teeth as they did so.

The Maera were bigger than normal wolves – they stood roughly the size of a lion or tiger. Long sharp spines jutted out of their backs and were now standing on end, marking their distress. Hyperion stopped a few paces from the steps to the large oak doors of the castle and turned to regard the snarling, growling creatures, raising his eyebrows in annoyance.

'What's the matter with you?' he asked as a group of shouting security guards and staff ran from around the base of the tower up the drive and away from something yet unseen by Hyperion.

They sprinted past him, oblivious to his presence, shrieking and gasping at the sight of the Maera. Hyperion remained still, puzzled, until he saw a dark form overtaking the lawn: it was a swarm of rats.

Just as he had noticed the rats, the oak doors to the castle opened and three more panicked security guards ran out, followed closely by a flowing multitude of rats piling on each other and spilling from the castle doors onto the gravel drive like a sea of wild fur.

Hyperion sneered in disgust and stared at the flowing black carpet of rats scampering towards him. But as the mass approached the king, it seamlessly split into two streams that flowed around him and the Maera, which hissed and snarled at the rats as they passed. Hyperion resumed his walk.

He entered the main hall and thereupon sat upon Taranis' throne without let or hindrance, or any moral hesitation. He glanced about the room admiring the suits of armour and various shields and weapons that adorned the walls.

Against one wall, a great marble fireplace with roaring flames cast insanely dancing shadows across the stone floor and wood-panelled walls. One of the Maera wasted no time in padding up to the hearth and settling down to sleep.

Another settled down by Hyperion's side, while the other two wandered with a sense of ownership, about the room, occasionally stopping to sniff at one of the suits of armour or other antiques that populated the hall.

'King Hyperion, sir, please do make yourself comfortable,' said a short, balding staff member as he scuttled into the hallway from one of the adjoining corridors. 'King Taranis has been made aware of your impressive presence and is on his way,' he said.

'Good,' King Summer dismissed him with a wave. One of the Maera trotted towards the attendant growling at him, causing the poor fellow to scurry from the grand hall as if his very life depended on it, which it probably did. *Where is that damned fool*? Hyperion wondered impatiently.

Meanwhile, Willow and Jacen ran headlong down a deserted corridor. Willow turned her head and glanced back to see a stream of rats scurrying after them. They burst into the room where Willow had been held a few days before as the rats scurried past.

Jacen glanced at Willow and burst out laughing. Willow and Jacen opened the door and peered into the corridor, and, seeing no one, continued.

They moved quickly but quietly along the corridor.

'Jacen stop. Someone's coming,' Willow hissed, pulling his arm. They pressed themselves into an alcove that had a suit of armour in it, only to see William and Heli in the corridor. Willow stepped out 'What are you two doing here?' she demanded to know.

'I couldn't stand it, at home worrying about you,' Heli said, 'I'm your Guardian Elf!'

'Same here. I was worried. Besides, I would have got one of Dad's "protect your sister" speeches if anything happened to you,' he shrugged.

'Come on then,' Willow shrugged. She was pleased but didn't want William to know that.

The castle appeared empty of all inhabitants, most likely evacuated en masse by the rodent event, and so the children had no trouble finding King Taranis' office.

It was the one with the huge desk and impressive chair. Jacen pulled a lesser, spare chair over to the desk and sat William down.

'You okay William,' Jacen asked, concerned.

The black edges in his vision threatened to overwhelm William. He raised his hand, unable to speak as he fought off the urge to faint. He had thought he was past this, but obviously not, he thought.

'Yeah, still not up to running,' he grimaced as Willow glared at him.

Jacen sat in the King's chair and tapped some keys making the screen light up. 'Darn it all to dammit, the computer has gone into stand-by with a password. We need to run a password cracker because we'll never guess it,' Jacen whispered.

'Well do it then. We need to see what's on this computer,' William whispered while the girls had a quick look in the filing cabinet against the far wall. Once satisfied there was nothing of relevant importance in it, they stood guard by the door.

'Just give me a few minutes and I will have this computer busted wide open,' said Jacen, cracking his knuckles. A few moments later Jason exclaimed, 'I am in!' with a big grin. 'Right then, time for the hard part,' he said, moving the mouse around the screen like an expert.

'We need something that proves us being here was no accident,' Heli hissed from her place by the door.

'Yes, look in his files and see if he has any information about us. Something he should not know, not just mundane stuff. See if he knows who Mum really is and if he plans to hurt her in some way' Willow chimed in.

'Ok I will see what I can do...um who is your mum?' Jacen frowned.

'Oh, trust me you wouldn't believe us if we told you,' William grinned.

After a few minutes searching through King Winter's mundane, and at times quite amusing documents, Jacen found what he was looking for.

'It looks like a FERA file all about Mum,' said William. 'Someone from the government told Taranis everything.' Willow passed Jacen the memory stick.

'What's FERA?' asked Jacen as he plugged the stick into the computer port download to copy the files.

'It's the Food and Environment Research Agency. Mum and Dad work for them occasionally,' William explained. using Heli to hear so he could talk to Jacen normally.

'Does it say who sent it?' Willow cut in.

'No, it doesn't,' William said. 'Copy everything in there, and we can check it all out later!'

'Right you are, boss.' Jacen grinned, pleased to have shown them to be the hacktivist genius he was reputed to be.

'Are you done?' called Heli from the door where she was keeping watch. 'I think someone's coming!'

'One more second,' both boys chimed, watching the bar quickly moving to show the download progress.

'We don't have the time. We need to go now!' Willow said as she heard the footsteps getting closer.

'Okay, I'm just logging off now,' Jacen called over his shoulder. He drummed his fingers on the desk waiting for the downloading to end.

'No wait! Look there's more – his accounts!' William pointed. 'They will tell us everything.'

'Okay, look at them quickly,' Willow begged from the door.

'Look at this,' Jacen said. 'Taranis has been buying into a load of random companies.'

'Why would the be doing that?' William asked. 'Boys, we have to go now!' Willow insisted.

'Alright, come on Will – let's get out of here,' Jacen said as the accounts finally finished copying to the memory stick. Jacen wiped any evidence they had been there, logged off the computer, took out the flash drive and they all ran from the office.

'Hey! You four!' Three security guards walked briskly up the corridor. 'Stop!'

'Run!' shouted Heli as she turned and hurtled back up the corridor followed closely by the others.

'Come on Will, can you run?' Willow linked her arm in William's and pulled him along.

'Yeah, I think so,' William lied. He felt awful. A film of perspiration broke out on his forehead. But he tried his best to be quick as Willow propelled him along the corridor after Heli and Jacen.

CHAPTER NINE

Taranis entered his throne room to see King Summer surrounded by the four menacing Maera. Their eyes shone a deep crimson. As Taranis approached Hyperion the Maera raised their spines and growled. They began pacing around King Summer, forming an impenetrable ring.

'What are those things doing in my castle?' Taranis demanded, glancing at them with distaste.

'Don't you like them?' Hyperion said, stroking the one nearest to him. 'The Summer Dark Elves gave them to me to show how grateful they were to our building operations. They are willing to do my bidding.' Hyperion looked pleased with himself.

'That doesn't answer the question of what they are doing here,' Taranis said, scowling at Hyperion.

'They are here as my personal security. It's good to have my entourage close by,' Hyperion smiled. 'Anyway, do you have her, is the Child of Nature here?' he asked eagerly.

'Yes, well, there have been some, erm...complications with the kidnapping,' Taranis paused. 'Her brother came along as well, with an Elf.'

'No matter,' said Hyperion. 'Take me to her. I want to see what she looks like.'

'Erm, about that...they...went home and Mother Nature came and thanked me for rescuing them.' Taranis grimaced at the rage erupting on Hyperion's face. He noticed the Maera growing more and more restless.

'I gave you one simple job and you've screwed it up.'

'I wasn't comfortable having them here. This is my home,' Taranis snapped back.

At that moment, a member of King Winter's security detail rushed in, interrupting their heated discussion. 'Sir, sir I must speak with you,' he blurted out. King Summer shot him a glance that could wilt an entire crop.

'What is it?' Taranis asked as the security guard noticed the animals for the first time and shrunk back in terror. The Maera made their way towards him and licked their chops.

'Someone has just...' His eyes darted toward the creatures as they edged closer, slinking across the floor. The guard swallowed, stepping back.

'Spit it out man, or has a wolf got your tongue?' Taranis raised his voice.

'...Logged into the computer in your office, sir,' the terrified peon said in a rush.

'What! Send a team there now and apprehend them!'

The guard saluted then gratefully and hurried from the room.

Meanwhile, not too far away, William leant against a wall, panting for breath. 'I can't run anymore,' he signed at Willow.

'You have to William,' Willow pleaded, putting her arm around him.

'Oi you two stay where you are!' the guard recently with Taranis shouted. He was jogging around the corner of the corridor.

'Go William, I can hold him up for a bit and give you time,' Willow hugged him and pushed him toward the door to the garden. She then made a fuss of tying her laces. As the guard got nearer, Willow jumped to her feet barging into him. She then hooked her foot round his leg and with another shove pushed him to the floor before running after William.

Jacen bolted out the door and down the corridor. He had no idea which way to go. He glanced over his shoulder to see a burly guard chasing him. Jacen just ran. He charged around the ground floor, passing shocked members of staff until he found an open window to climb out. He soon caught up with Heli and grabbed her hand pulling her along.

A little while later, the bruised and anxious, and hapless, security guard returned. 'Sir, we almost caught them leaving your office, but they split up and ran. We think they are trying to escape through the grounds. It's the children that were visiting the other day.' The guard panted, his chest heaving from the exertion of the chase. He held his elbow where Willow had knocked him to the floor earlier.

'Really how unexpectedly interesting,' mused Taranis. 'They only need to make it to the woods, and we'll have lost them, again.'

'No,' Hyperion spoke after a pause. 'We won't. We'll just send these after them.' King Hyperion turned to the Maera. 'Go! Hurt them if you must, but bring the girl back alive – do you understand? Now go!' With that, the Maera barked demonically and sped out the oak doors.

'We may rectify your incompetence after all,' Hyperion smiled.

Not realising the terrible pursuers on his trail, Jacen sprinted across the lawn, yanking Heli along. He was young, in good shape, and could run for England. He used every bit of power his muscles and lungs could muster. He glanced over his shoulder. To his horror he saw a great beast charging after them.

'Heli, we need to run faster,' he gasped.

'I can't,' Heli panted.

William and Willow were getting close to the wood. Jacen saw William stumble as another great beast neared him. Jacen was sure he could smell the disgusting hellish breath of the creature that was behind him. *Oh no, it's curtains*! Jacen thought desperately, as the leading wolf thing pounced straight at him. It was then that Willow and William crossed into the forest, and Jacen and Heli tumbled behind them.

'Help us!' Willow cried as William dropped to the ground. Tree Sprites appeared. One of them leapt up in the air and intercepted the leading Maera who slammed against a tree.

The rest of the Sprites jumped from their trees onto the Maera as if riding a hideous bucking bronco.

'Go! Get out of here now!' shouted a Sprite with all the energy of a Glasgow bouncer, to the children, just as one of the Maera leapt and latched its jaws around the Sprite's head. The Sprite was unperturbed, however, and slipped its long sharp fingers between the creature's ribs.

William watched the fight unfold between the variously strange and powerful creatures with nervous fascination as he waited for Willow to open the traveling portal in an oak tree.

Heli grabbed him and Jacen, while Willow held onto Heli's shoulder and reached out to touch the tree she had selected. With a flash of yellow light, the screams, shrieks, and growls around them dissolved. The children found themselves back underneath the apple tree in the garden behind their home!

'Phew! That was a close one,' Jacen said, breathing a sigh of relief. 'Beats EasyJet!'

'What were those things?' William asked.

'The dog creatures were Maera,' Heli explained. 'Very powerful and wicked things. Though what they were doing there, I do not know.'

'Come on, let's go see if Mum's here so we can show her the memory stick.'

****

Taranis smirked as one of King Summer's Maera came limping back into the hall. 'Evidently your pets were not up to the simple task of apprehending a few children,' Taranis said, turning to King Hyperion, who grimaced with a look of cold fury.

'Well, if you hadn't been so stupid as to put the children in the guest room instead of the dungeon, "my pets" wouldn't have had to do it in the first place!' Hyperion snapped.

'What do we do now?' Taranis looked at the whimpering and bloodied Maera with disgust.

'They will be much harder to kidnap now,' said Hyperion. 'Not to mention that Mother

Nature will be particularly annoyed that we tried to steal her kids.'

'Indeed,' said Taranis, turning to Hyperion.

'We will just have to be more insistent. I have some friends who will be perfect for the job,' King Hyperion said, striding towards the exit of the castle.

The remaining Maera growled as it slowly limped behind Hyperion.

'And dispose of this would you?' Hyperion said, looking disloyally over his shoulder at the wounded animal before walking away.

At that moment, the children entered the kitchen to find it empty. William sat with his arms slumped on the table, his head resting on them.

'So much for the welcome home, glad you escaped the clutches of the evil Winter Elves et cetera, et cetera, et cetera ...' said William, annoyed.

Willow hid a smile. 'I don't mind that Mum isn't here. I rather enjoy being home alone and not having to fight over the TV remote – and being able to play my music really loud.'

'Well, I don't know about you guys, but I could eat a wolf I'm starving,' said Jacen, as he got up and walked to the fridge. He peered inside. 'Oh! Yuck!' he said. 'I forgot your Mum was one of those veggie types. Don't you lot ever eat proper junk food?' Jacen rummaged through the shelves and pulled out some cheese and a jar of pickles.

'This will just have to do,' Jacen said, his tone resigned. 'Cheese and pickle sandwich anyone?'

'No thanks, I think I'm gonna go to bed. I still feel a bit off – and all that running didn't help,' muttered William.

'William, are you alright?' Willow got up and felt his head. William pushed her hand away crossly.

'I'm fine! Leave me alone. I'm just a bit tired,' he snapped.

'You're not hungry, then?' said Willow, both surprised and worried. 'I read somewhere that people who hit their head could have mood swings.' But then again, this could just be his normal grumpy self, she thought.

'Stay where you are young man,' Lilly walked into the kitchen followed by Althea. 'Where may I ask have you been, and don't say Jacen's because I have just come back from there.' She glared at them all.

'We just went out for a bit,' Willow lied, gazing anywhere but at her mother.

'William, and think before you answer carefully, where have you been?' Lilly glared at him.

'We went back to the castle,' Willow blurted out.

'You did what?' Lilly rounded on her daughter.

'We went back to the castle Mum because we didn't get there last time by accident, and we had to find proof. And yes, we know it was stupid and dangerous, but we did find evidence,' William said as fast as he could, signing at the same time.

Lilly took a deep breath and pulled out a chair. 'Explain it to me,' she said.

'We think that the tree was meant to take us to the castle in Scotland. That we were being kidnapped by King Winter and were supposed to end up there. We think that because William came along when he shouldn't have, the tree got confused and sent us to slightly the wrong place.'

'She has a point Lilly, we could ask the tree,' Althea said telepathically.

'How did Jacen get there?' Lilly asked.

'Oh, um I got him…he um helped us get this,' Willow produced the hard-won memory stick.

'Let me show you what's on it Mrs. Milbank,' Jacen suggested.

'Okay,' Lilly said.

They went into the study where Jacen plugged in the device.

'My goodness, do you mind if I have this?' Lilly asked Jacen, after glancing at the files the computer displayed.

'No, we did it for you,' Jacen smiled.

'Willow go and tell your father that you're here. He's down in Greenhouse Two.'

'Yes Mum, and Mum sorry for worrying you,' Willow said.

'You're still grounded Willow,' Lilly smiled.

'Yes Mum,' Willow mumbled as she went to find her dad.

'William, I know you were only looking out for your sister, but you shouldn't be out of bed and that is where you're going now,'

Lilly admonished William as he got to his feet. 'I will send Willow up to wake you for dinner.'

'Yes Mum,' William answered as he shuffled out the kitchen.

Then, looking to Jacen: 'And you, young man are to stay here. Your mother guessed you were out with Willow. You know you can say no to her, Jacen, you don't have to go along with all her crazy ideas.' Lilly knew she was wasting her breath. She knew the boy would follow Willow to the ends of the earth.

'I know Ma'am,' Jacen answered.

It was at that point that Willow returned and sat at the kitchen table next to Jacen. 'Dad's on his way, said he would be here in a minute.'

'Fine, you two just wait here and stay out of trouble,' Lilly replied before walking out of the kitchen.

****

Jacen and Willow sat in the kitchen munching on a coffee cake.

'Well, that was an extremely exciting day, probably the best yet in your company,' remarked Jacen. 'Tomorrow is going to be sheer dishwater in comparison.'

'Well, my day won't be any better, you know,' said Willow. 'I will have to spend it with grumpy William because Mum thinks he's delicate, and we are grounded. So, we won't be allowed out, not even to see you.'

'Him, delicate, you are joking?' Heli chimed in and Willow shook her head laughing. Just then the front door opened, and David walked in. He looked relieved at the sight of the children, until he noticed one was still missing.

'Where is your brother?' David asked, looking around the kitchen in panic.

'He's gone back to bed. Today has all been too much for him,' Willow said.

'Well, I think it's time I saw Jacen home – and you, young lady, need a bath. And it would not hurt you to have an early night either,' David said, using his best *I'm your father voice*.

'Bye, Willow,' Jacen gave Willow an awkward hug. 'See you in the week,' Jacen called as

David hustled him through the front door and along the path to the car. Willow waved, as she watched the car's taillights disappear down the lane into the fading twilight.

CHAPTER TEN

Lilly sat at her desk in her office at FERA peering at her computer screen, with Althea. Although it did function in its official capacity as a research agency it was also a front, designed and created with the actual purpose of helping Mother Nature with her duties. These duties included the careful monitoring and coordination of the changing of the seasons. Not to mention keeping the Elven world hidden from Human knowledge, and acting as an ambassador between them; or, for that matter, holding back the environmental catastrophe that global warming and general pollution from Human expansion had caused over the last few centuries.

At that moment however Lilly and Althea had suspended their usual tasks, delegating them to other members of their team so that they could spend the morning studying the information on the infamous Scottish memory stick.

'Althea, my eyes are starting to hurt,' Lilly commented, rubbing her temples.

'This is massively complicated. What is he up to?' Althea squinted at the screen.

'I have no idea, but I am beginning to think Willow is right, and the kids being at the castle was no accident. But why would Taranis want my children? What could he possibly gain?' Lilly rubbed her temples again.

'We should go to Lord Hurleston,' Althea said. 'We're going need his help.'

Lilly winced at the idea. Lord Hurleston was the aging, no nonsense, putative head of FERA.

'You're probably right, but what should I say to get him on board?' Lilly examined the stolen stick in her hand. *Should I use it?*

'Well Child of Nature was put in jeopardy. Surely her protection is paramount,' Althea interjected.

'Was she though? I mean, yes I know she was, but when you think about it, or tell someone else, it does at first glance look like a little tree accident,' Lilly half-smiled.

'What about the mist?' Althea interjected.

'I have no proof that did or did not happen. That is the problem – I have no real proof.

Who is going to believe a couple of impetuous teenagers against King Winter?'

'I see your dilemma,' Althea gazed into space, thinking.

'I know Taranis is plotting against me – but why? I realise that the Fairy community has been unhappy for a while now, but there's hardly anything I can do about the current situation.'

'Well, it's not like they had much of a choice, was it?' Althea said. 'And anyway, for the most part it worked out quite well for the Elves. I mean look at the Summer Elves – they are thriving as are the Spring and Winter Elves. They have integrated into Human society seamlessly. It's only the Autumn Elves that keep to themselves and there are so few of them it's not really a problem,' Althea shrugged.

Lilly felt her scalp prickle. Something else is going on here, she thought to herself. 'It's just not like King Taranis to suddenly turn on me like this. I wonder if he's acting alone or if someone else is involved…goading him on.' Lilly paused and gazed at Althea who shrugged. 'And if that is the case, then who exactly? Not all the Elder Council, I hope – and what about the Queens? Are they involved in the vast conspiracy too?'

'I doubt that,' Althea said. 'Queen Winter definitely isn't helping Taranis – and we'd have heard something if Queen Alectrona or Queen Andarta were unhappy. Although to be fair Queen Andarta has been miserable for the last few decades,' Althea giggled, making Lilly smile.

'In that case maybe Taranis *is* working alone. Things might not be so bad.' Lilly sighed, 'As if I'm not busy enough without that twit acting up as well, we're meant to be in Japan by the end of the week to help assess the damage out there.'

'We can probably afford to delay that a week or two,' said Althea. 'The Japanese seem to have managed preventing a complete meltdown. It is just a case of determining whether Reactor Four is ruptured and leaking radiation. And if it is, there's not too much we can do about it.'

'Hmm,' Lilly said, leaning back in her chair. 'You're right.'

She bound to her feet. 'Come on, let us go and show this to Lord Hurleston.'

To her surprise, the door to his office opened just before she got there, and Gail walked out. He was dressed in a smart suit which made him appear far older than his nineteen years. He was escorted out by Laran, King Autumn. Gail's brown almost black eyes seemed to survey her with slight amusement.

Lilly often saw Gail around. He worked in the department, and she would see him in the cafeteria or chatting to other members of staff in the corridor or by the water cooler and it occurred to her that she had never spoken to him.

King Autumn turned and surveyed Althea before his gaze drifted. He seemed to be looking at something further down the corridor. He stopped and smiled. 'Mother Nature! It's good to see you,' he said, eyes crinkling at the corners as he smiled.

A slight blush stole across Lilly's cheeks as she took in his features, from his combed almost curly auburn hair to the hint of stubble along his perfect jawline. *Good grief this man is attractive, and I need to stop behaving like a schoolgirl* she thought, taking a deep breath. Lilly noticed wrinkles etched around his striking, dark emerald eyes and upon his brow, suggesting that he spent a lot of time either laughing or frowning. Her interactions with him had been minimal over the years so she hardly knew the man, she mainly dealt with his second, Hàlfr and she often thought that was intentional as if he were avoiding her. Despite being a key member of the Elder Council, she cannot have seen him more than twice before and had never spoken to him directly. Lilly brushed that thought aside as she answered his question.

'It's good to see you too, King Laran of Autumn,' Lilly said. Of all the Kings, Lilly found Laran the easiest to work with, his team accommodating and efficient even if the man himself was absent.

'Please just Laran I hate the King bit,' he grinned.

'Oh, right,' Lilly paused 'I...haven't seen you or Queen Andarta for a while. Everything alright?'

'Yes, fine. We have just been incredibly busy planning for the autumn season and because of the constant threat from The Dark

Elves,' Laran explained, running his hand through his hair.

Lilly stood still and waited as King Laran continued. 'The Dark Elves have begun another offensive and this one's worse than the others. I was just informing Lord Hurleston of the situation. He likes to stay informed as these Elves are just as likely to attack Humans as they are to attack their own kind.' King Laran spoke in a quiet, commanding voice.

As this handsome man spoke, Gail raised his eyebrows at Althea, who stared at him.

'May I enquire what brings you to Lord Hurleston's office?' King Laran asked, taking in every detail of Lilly's appearance.

Lilly was no slouch in the looks department either: she wore a soft silk, muted-blue round neck blouse, which was slightly open at the neck, suggestively professional. A grey Armani pencil skirt hugged her hips. A slightly darker blue sweater from Chanel draped her shoulders. She was wearing a hint of makeup to mask the fact that she had not slept properly over the last couple of days. Her lips had been lip-sticked incarnadine. She presented the consummate picture of a 'yummy mummy' – a beautiful, smart, capable woman in command of her appearance and style.

'Oh! just some teenage problems – although that probably doesn't sound really important.' Lilly stumbled over her words, tucking a stray piece of hair behind her ear. 'What I mean is, Willow has been behaving oddly, gaining her gifts earlier than anticipated, then William had an accident, and I don't know, it reminded me of something else that had been nagging at me, but I just couldn't put my finger on it – an instinct I suppose,' she said with a weak smile.

'How is young William? Not too badly hurt, I hope?' Laran asked, his brow creasing in a frown, his green eyes darkening with concern.

'Oh, Yes! He's fine – always been a bit delicate, that one,' Lilly said. 'And Willow can be a little rough with him at times. You know, kids.'

'Indeed,' said Laran. 'Well, I can't keep you here talking all day.' He turned to Gail. 'This fine young gentleman was just showing me out and I'm sure you are eager to discuss your teenager troubles with Lord Hurleston,' he chuckled and turned to walk down the corridor towards the elevator.

Lilly stood in the corridor watching him leave. *Why had she said those stupid things? Why had she said anything?* It could have just been a nice, civilised conversation instead of that awkward attempt at idiotic small talk. Lilly castigated herself as she walked into the waiting room to Lord Hurleston's CEO-style office.

'Can you tell him I'm here to see him, please?' she asked the receptionist.

'He's free right now if you'd like to go straight through,' the receptionist, Mary Appleton, replied.

'Thank you,' Lilly said as she did just that. Hurleston looked perfectly groomed as he sat behind his desk, typing away. He was slightly older than her, with salt and pepper hair, vintage designer glasses from London, and expensive taste in clothes. Rumour had it all his suits were tailored just for him, using only the finest silk threads. He also favoured rare and exotic perfumes from Paris, often combining hints of floral extracts with more 'masculine' ingredients, including sweat and tobacco.

'Aah! Mother Nature how are you?' he motioned towards the chair by his desk. 'You look tired.'

'Thanks. The same could be said for you,' Lilly said, sitting down. 'Dark Elves been troubling you again?'

'Yes,' Hurleston said, his expression suddenly serious as the grave. 'Somehow they've managed to identify and kill five of my agents since the start of the year. Before this, we could only trace about one or two Human killings back to Dark Elf involvement – and that was over five or more years ago. Something has really riled them,' Hurleston said with a sigh. 'We narrowly managed to stop them derailing a train the other day – can you imagine that? A train! Full of people! Imagine if they had gotten away with it? How would I explain that to the PM?' Hurleston leaned back in his chair. He almost looked offended, as though all this might somehow be Lilly's fault.

'Well, I wish I had some good news for you, but things are a little worse than even you think,' Lilly replied. 'It appears that King Winter has been conspiring to kidnap my children and almost got one killed.'

'I assume that he didn't succeed and that your children are safe now?' Lord Hurleston asked.

'Yes, they are thank you,' Lilly responded curtly and paused, unsure how to phrase what she wanted to say next. After a moment's hesitation, Lilly decided to just say it. 'Look, I think I know how the Dark Elves are singling out your agents...and I think Taranis is working alongside somebody in the Dark Elves' camp.'

'Do you know any of this for certain?' Lord Hurleston asked, looking alarmed.

'No, not yet – but I do know that there is definitely a spy working for them within FERA who has been passing along confidential information, including a file that compromises me.'

Lord Hurleston pressed his fingers together, like a steeple desperately requiring a religion. He looked worried. 'And how do you know this?'

Lilly pulled out the all-important memory stick from her pocket. 'When the children were in King Winter's castle, they broke into his computer and downloaded a load of his files.'

At this, Lord Hurleston sat up straight, alarmed. 'They did what?' Lord Hurleston barked. 'Lilly, have you any idea what will happen if Taranis finds out about this? You are aware that stealing his files was a crime, and that by accepting them from your children you too are culpable?'

'Well kidnapping isn't strictly legal either,' Lilly retorted.

'Yes, but from what I have heard, they were not held forcibly now, were they? How certain are you that it was a kidnapping and not just a silly accident of Willow's?' Lord Hurleston peered at Lilly from under his thick, knitted brows. 'If that is the case – if it indeed is an accident – you are indebted to King Winter for taking them in and looking after them.'

'What?' Lilly replied, dumbfounded by his sudden change of tone.

'Any evidence towards it being a kidnapping is merely circumstantial – while this is hard evidence that you stole King Winter's property. Need I remind you that King Winter is particularly wealthy and therefore can afford the best lawyers. The Elder Council has demonstrated before that they are not afraid to carry out aggressive litigation and in this financial climate, we simply cannot afford that.'

'But they are dangerous, and we have to stop them,' Lilly said. 'I am Mother Nature. The Kings and Queens ultimately answer to me and they know this. Kidnapping my children – no matter how well they treat them – is completely unacceptable and we need to show them that,' Lilly spluttered, annoyed that the conversation had taken such a turn.

'I agree,' said Lord Hurleston, 'but this evidence cannot be used against them. I will task some of my best people with keeping tabs on Taranis.' Lord Hurleston paused. 'Apart from that, there is not much I can do...And as for this alleged spy, until we have a better idea of who it is, if they exist, it's far too risky to try and do anything about it. We must be certain, to know who we can trust.'

'Spoken like a true mandarin, Lord Hurleston – but we have to show Taranis that he cannot get away with this sort of thing,' Lilly said.

'He needs to know that as Mother Nature, I'm the one in charge and you have to help me get that message across.' Lilly stood up, fuming.

'I'm afraid I cannot help you. There is simply nothing that I or this department can do at this point,' Lord Hurleston said. 'Might I suggest, if you really oversee them, you get your own house in order without our help. Surely there are still some members of the Elder Council who can help you. Now go home – and tomorrow you must come to work as if nothing is wrong. I'm sure your lovely grandmother can watch the children.'

Lilly had entered a state of utter shock, and even though her mouth dropped open and closed repeatedly, neither words nor counter arguments came out.

'Now unless there is more you wish to discuss with me?' he said, pompously, as if trying out for the part of a sexist pale and stale boomer boss in a new Sitcom, raising his eyebrows and looking up at her in a manner that made it certain that he considered the matter closed.

'No,' replied Lilly, regaining her composure, and gritting her teeth. 'That's all, for now.'

She turned around and strutted out defiantly, closely followed by Althea, who had been silent the whole time.

'That was pretty intense huh?' Althea commented telepathically.

'I can't believe he's going to do nothing about this. I thought the entire point of FERA was to help me do my job,' Lilly raged as they walked along the modern top floor of FERA, between glass walled offices towards the lifts.

'He does kind of have a point though, you haven't really interacted much with King Taranis at all. I think it's time you really flexed your muscles as Mother Nature...figuratively speaking of course,' Althea commented.

'Are you kidding? Openly testing King Taranis could lead to another Ice Age. Also, what image does that project about me to the other Kings and Queens, let alone the Elven houses? They'd just see me as some power-crazed despot pushing them around,' Lilly replied as the lifts arrived. They stepped in, keying the button for the infirmary in the basement.

'I think despot's a bit strong, but I get your point. Do you have an alternative?' Althea asked as the doors closed and the lift began to descend.

'We're going to have to try and talk some sense into him, and that will be a lot easier if we had some of the other Kings and Queens on our side. Plus, if it does come to an open confrontation, it would look a lot better if our actions are endorsed or supported by some of the others.'

'Yes, but what if they are helping him? How do we know who to trust? The corridors of Elven power are pretty internecine and Byzantine at the best of times,' Althea observed as the lift doors opened to reveal the solitary tree growing in the entrance of FERA's infirmary.

'I bet Queen Winter isn't helping him as far as he can throw a Frisbee, and I have a feeling that if King Autumn were involved, I would have sensed it...He's a tricky one. I want to trust him, but I am not entirely comfortable around him, something about him feels slightly off. His whole *noblesse oblige* act and obvious use of Handsome Pills is a bit of a dead giveaway. I don't know, let's go home and I'll think about it some more.'

'You know, he was rumoured to have been involved in your mother's death. Maybe it is time you read the file,' Althea suggested gently.

'I have heard the rumours. Maybe I should?' Lilly answered, as she outstretched her hand towards the tree and the pair of them vanished in a flash of golden light.

As they departed, Gail walked along the corridor on the fifteenth floor of the FERA building with his dad. The meeting with Lord Hurleston had been interesting but not highly informative. Lord Hurleston seemed to say a lot, but it all meant nothing – quite a clever technique. *Typical politician,* Gail thought.

'So, Dad – that was Mother Nature,' Gail mused as they stepped into the lift.

'Yes, that she was. What did you think?' Laran smiled.

'Um, she was a lot younger than I expected. She finds you intimidating – despite the fact she finds you attractive,' Gail smiled as Laran rolled his eyes and sighed.

'Half the office fancies you, Dad. And the other half fancies her, including you. She is cute…but there is something else about her…' Gail paused while thinking. 'Danger – she has a dangerous air about her. Under that sweet vulnerable exterior there is steel. You can hear it in her voice. I wouldn't want to cross her.' Gail grinned 'I can see why you like her.'

'Very perceptive, son. Harvard was lucky to have you. Yeah, I find her attractive – all that power contained in such a delicate little thing,' Laran mused. 'You should have met her mother. Wow.'

'Dad!' Gail laughed, surprised at his father's candour.

'Anything else?' Laran asked, impressed at Gail's judgement of character.

'How old are the children?' Gail asked.

'Um, William is eighteen and Willow is fourteen – almost fifteen,' Laran answered as they stepped out of the lift and walked across the lobby into the street.

'Not really children at all, then,' Gail said.

'I suppose not. Legally, yes. Grown up enough to get into dangerous scrapes and push at the boundaries of the known universe with questions eons old. Never underestimate them. Willow is Child of Nature, so must be protected. There are plenty of people and Elves who do not like Mother Nature, and what she represents to certain powers that be, and would not think twice about harming her. And I believe William has a certain vulnerability,' Laran explained, his tone clipped. 'How is the headache?' Laran glanced at Gail, changing the subject.

'Better thanks,' Gail fixed a questioning gaze on his father.

'She doesn't know about the psychic link between William and I, does she?'

'Come on, psychic is a bit strong, sometimes he stubs his toe, and you feel it, you can hardly read his mind,' Laran replied.

'That is not the point, doesn't she have a right to know? You're basically spying on them.'

'Obviously at some point I'll tell her, but right now the time isn't right for it,' Laran responded authoritatively.

'Oh good,' Gail said. 'Feel free to inform me when you do decide to tell her. Right,' Gail said, clearing his throat. 'Where are we going for dinner? You're buying.'

END OF BOOK ONE

BOOK TWO CONTINUES THE TALE OF THE SEASONS SERIES!

Lightning Source UK Ltd.
Milton Keynes UK
UKHW040741070521
383278UK00002B/189